D0687267

SENSELESS

OTHER TITLES BY STONA FITCH

Strategies for Success

SENSELESS

For Dave—

Stona Fitch

[signature]

SOHO

Published by
Soho Press, Inc.
853 Broadway
New York, NY 10003

Library of Congress Cataloging-in-Publication Data

Fitch, Stona.
Senseless : a novel / Stona Fitch.
p. cm.
ISBN 1-56947-268-8 (alk. paper)
1. Victims of terrorism—Fiction. 2. Torture victims—Fiction.
3. Kidnapping—Fiction 4. Internet—Fiction. 5. Belgium—Fiction. I. Title.

PS3556.I816S462001
813'.54—dc21   2001042047

DESIGNED BY KATHLEEN LAKE, NEUWIRTH AND ASSOCIATES, INC.

Manufactured in the United States of America
10   9   8   7   6   5 4 3   2   1

For Ann
J.A.T.H.

"He should not perceive sound with his ears, nor feel touch with his skin. He should not perceive form with his eyes, taste with his tongue, nor gather scents from the wind. He should courageously reject the five agitators of the senses."

—The Mahabharata

"Power resides in the moment of transition from a past to a new state."

—Emerson

Picture the room where you will be held captive. You know there is one—everyone carries this room with them. A basement room from your childhood, shelves cluttered with forgotten toys and yellowed files. A classroom from your student days, each wall lined with blank blackboards. A bright apartment with a view of the city, the night avenues glistening with rain. The corner room of an old hotel, the glass transom over the door half open. Any room can become a prison. All it takes is a key and someone to turn it. Perhaps you will do the turning yourself.

My father spent his days in the cell of his choice—a fine office in a sandstone building on the outskirts of Roanoke. My mother was high-strung and had trouble staying in the house for long. The sight of one insignificant item missing from our household would send her on a series of interlocking errands that could last all day. As a boy, I was a poor student and painfully shy, a combination that sent me into hiding with ailments more imaginary than

1

chronic. I often found myself at home, reading in my bed, soup cooling on a wooden tray next to a tall glass of flat Coca-Cola laced with brandy, my mother's universal remedy.

I would close the door to my room and imagine myself confined not by illness or false illness, but by someone else. Bart, the blond bully from school with his huge hands and dead gray eyes. Or my father, perpetually frustrated with the laziness he found in me and my brother Darby. It could be him behind the door, turning the key and holding me in my room until I learned to respect all the blessings that we had been given. The captor wasn't important. It was the prisoner who concerned me.

I had read tales of pioneers held by Indian tribes, soldiers imprisoned in Andersonville, criminals stranded on the rock island of Alcatraz. The small scale of their lives entranced me the way that lead soldiers had when I was younger and that astronauts would when I was older. It fascinated me that an entire world could be confined to a small place, that the Battle of Culloden Moor could be reenacted on the living-room rug, that three men could live and work in a capsule even smaller than my room. Through these boundaries I learned the virtue of restraint, always the quiet boy's excuse for not hurtling headfirst into the world.

When the light faded, giving way to the slow gray winter afternoon, I would leave the lamps off, waiting in the dark to see who would be the first to come home. My father returning from the office. My mother back from her errands. My brother done with football practice. Each would enter our house with footsteps of varying strengths. My father's boots thumped along as he went from room to room turning on lamps. My brother's cleats stayed only in the kitchen, where he stood in front of the open refrigerator and scanned its contents. My mother's heels clicked like a metronome. Eventually, one would climb the stairs to my room and twist the knob to find it locked.

In my room, I would stare, paralyzed, at the rattling brass knob. My captor had arrived, bringing food and water, a scolding, presents, further confinement. Which would it be this time? Then I would break the spell and walk slowly toward the door, reaching up to throw the deadbolt that would let them in, let me out. As the door swung open, the prison walls would vanish as quickly as they had been created and I would be set free. But on another day, behind another door, a new captor waited along the golden horizon, for fear attracts its object as surely as desire. With my imaginary confinements, I set the stage for another, more peculiar imprisonment.

DAY 1. I met a group of software executives for dinner at Le Nez Fin, an elegant new restaurant just off the Grand-Place, not far from my office in Brussels. Filet de boeuf with black truffle reduction, stoemp sweated in goose fat, potée bruxelloise, and bottle after bottle of wine crowded the corner table where our group huddled. I identified the Pommard, the Vosne-Romanée, and the Chambolle-Musigny even when Monsieur Tas, the foreign marketing director, switched the glasses. They were impressed that an American could be so attuned to nuance. Years in Washington, London, and Brussels had left me rarefied.

I spent much of my career at parties, dinners, receptions. My field was not theoretical. I was not tucked away in an ivory tower. I was out in the world, imperfect though it might be. Our table was the setting for careful intertwining of European and American interests. Our conversation turned now and then to various technologies that could be transferred given the right conditions and other enticements to trade. I never thought in coarse terms of deals or contracts. I was simply a liaison. I brought the right people together the way an expert host does. Others in my organization endured interminable meetings in The Hague or Geneva. Most of my time was spent in restaurants and hotels, environments where I truly flourished, a night-blooming flower.

Many hours after we entered, our group of six emerged from the restaurant, sated as honeybees in August. I must have had at least a bottle of wine plus a brandy with my coffee. I was not drunk, but thrumming with the heightened awareness that I often sensed walking the streets of Brussels in the blue hours close to dawn. I smelled the damp cobblestones, sour gutter rot, cigarette smoke clinging to empty cafés. Seen walking toward my apartment on Avenue Louise that morning—and I suppose I was being observed—I would have worn a bleary half-smile of contentment, blue overcoat pulled tight around my waist, collar turned up against the chill of an early fall.

I can't recall when I first noticed the grating tires on the road behind me. I thought for a moment that one of my dinner companions had driven up to offer me a lift back to my apartment. As I turned, someone rushed up behind me and pulled a pillowcase over my head. It happened so fast that I didn't even think to fight the hands pushing me forward. Footsteps on the cobblestones. The click of a key in a lock. In seconds, I was in the trunk, my head banging against a spare tire as the car sped away. I pulled off the hood, gasping. In the darkness, my mind raced and I fought the rising panic.

The car bumped through the night. Cobblestones gave way to highway and I sensed that we were on the ring road around the centrum. I tried to count the turns, the lefts and rights and stops. But there were too many. The air in the trunk warmed and turned stale. I recalled that there were cars with emergency latches in the trunk. I groped around but couldn't find one. And what good would it have done me? The tires hummed on the road just beneath me.

After about an hour, the car stopped suddenly. I heard the doors open. Keys rattled and the trunk opened, hands reached in quickly to pull the pillowcase back over my face. They lifted me out and stood me on my feet.

"Here, take my wallet." I fumbled in my jacket pocket.

A hard fist to my stomach was their only answer. I curled around it, the pain ending any illusion that this was all a joke. They hoisted me like a bag of sand and carried me a few feet. It took four men to carry such an awkward load and I could hear them straining. After a few feet, they dropped me unceremoniously on the gritty metal floor. The doors of a freight elevator slammed closed, then the elevator shook slightly. In a minute, the elevator stopped. The door opened and a kick to the small of my back pushed me forward. I stumbled and fell on the concrete floor. The doors closed again. Pressed against the cold cement, I listened, sensing that I was alone again. I struggled out of the pillowcase and turned. I ran to the wall. The space between the elevator doors was almost seamless. I tried to pry them apart, then slapped my hand against them. A small metallic echo ricocheted down the elevator shaft.

"Stop!" I shouted, then realized I was probably better off alone. I walked back into the room.

I found myself in a clean, empty apartment. The walls were painted painfully white and the room seemed half-finished, with the metal doorframes unpainted, small ducts poking from the high ceiling. The plate-glass windows of the first room, a large living room, were painted white as well, diffusing the dim morning light. I ran my fingernail across the window but couldn't scratch the paint away. I walked through the open door to the adjoining room. In it, I saw a futon on the floor, new and smelling of plastic wrapping. Next to the futon was a carton of mineral water in liter bottles.

Nothing indicated that this apartment was prepared specifically for me. No one had called me by name. I assumed that they had mistaken me for someone else. I had been in the wrong place in the early hours of the morning, looking prosperous. I had read reports of *pesca milagrosa* in Colombia. *Miraculous fishing.* Roadblocks stopped all cars, weeding out the wealthy travelers like fat fish from a pond. Miraculous for the fisherman, less so for the fish. But this was Brussels, the polite heart of Europe. In any case, what would they think when they found out they had they caught only a mid-level American economist with relatively little money and even less power?

The two windows in the bedroom were also painted white. I managed to pull away a paintbrush bristle that had been embedded in the thick paint, removing a line of paint barely wider than a hair. I took a 20-franc piece from my pocket and scraped it along the hairline to widen it slightly. Squinting close to the line, I could see that this room faced the other side of the building, which was shaped like the letter *E* with the middle stroke removed. Far below, I could make out an indistinct, hazy landscape and the brick smokestacks of factories. I guessed we were on the outskirts of Antwerp, but I couldn't be sure.

I walked back through the living room to the third room in the flat. I scraped a tiny paint blister with my coin and peered through, seeing only the whitewashed windows of the bedroom I had just been in. This room was empty except for two black metal folding chairs placed facing each other. Adjoining it was a small bathroom with a shower, sink, and toilet. The tilework and plumbing looked as if it had been completed hours before my arrival. All of the rooms smelled sharp with plaster and paint.

I paced around the three rooms and tried to summon up my training from so many years ago. More than thirty years had passed, time and neglect winnowing down what I once knew. *When you are taken, you must remain calm. To ensure your safety and eventual release, you must try to engage those who hold you in a dialog.* There was something else about how the negotiations had to work from two directions, from the embassy and from the hostage. But I had forgotten anything useful.

Hostage. What an alien word it seemed at the time. Dimly from my training, I remembered that the key to avoiding fear—which made even the strongest man vulnerable—meant sidestepping any thoughts of potential danger. It was important to stay focused on the moment, on what one had, rather than what one was being denied.

I was in a clean apartment large enough for a family. I had water, air, and light. I had a comfortable place to sleep. I even had a bathroom. For now, this would have to be enough. I lay on the futon and closed my eyes, giving in to sleep for a few moments. It was five in the morning. On any other day I would have been asleep in my apartment, comfortable, safe.

DAY 2. I woke at midmorning sure that I was at home on our farm in Virginia. When I opened my eyes I saw a black wire ending in a small bulb no bigger than a scallion. It swayed slightly just above my face, a small red light glowing. I grabbed at the wire but it quickly retracted up into one of the ceiling ducts, an electrical snake. I stood on the carton of water bottles and ran my hand up in the duct but found nothing. I walked into the bathroom and splashed water on my face, then rubbed my hands through my hair. I wondered whether someone watched me from the other side of the bathroom mirror. I pressed two quick crescents into the plaster next to the sink with my thumb to mark my time here.

All the while, I stared into the mirror. The whites of my eyes were cloudy from last night, the flesh beneath them gray as an oyster. The skein of shallow wrinkles stretched around my eyes like crazing on an old vase. But in the familiar constellation of lines, moles, and discolorations, I saw nothing new, no sign that I was not the same person I was yesterday, though I was no longer free. Freedom denied doesn't show itself on the surface, like worry or fatigue or anger. It resided somewhere other than the face.

I wet my hands and ran them through my hair, graying but still thick and cut rather short. When we lived in London, I was occasionally mistaken for John Hurt, the British actor. I took this mistake as a compliment, but didn't like being noticed. Being singled out was one of my childhood fears, that father would have me speak at the dinner table, that a teacher at Groton would call on me to discuss the cetology chapter of *Moby-Dick*. My goal then, as now, was to be unnoticed, invisible.

As I walked into the bedroom, I saw a paper bag next to the carton of water bottles. Had this been here all along? Or had someone come in while I slept and left it here? I wasn't sure. I opened it and found only a single apple. I examined it for pinpricks or any other sign that it had been tampered with or drugged but found none. I was very hungry. Had I been at the office, I would already have stepped out for bread and coffee. I bit into the crisp apple and tasted its sweetness, almost too sweet. I finished it off in a few bites, then repeated a habit from childhood and ate the core as well, chewing the seeds to a wooden pulp, leaving only the stem. My mother had always joked that I would wind up with a forest in my stomach.

I laughed, then wondered if I was still being watched, what they would make of their hostage sitting on the floor of an empty room, laughing at nothing.

I spent the morning pacing around the three rooms, settling finally in the one farthest from where I had slept. I arranged the contents of my pocket on the floor. A wallet. A silver pen given to me for twenty-five years with IBIS. Several receipts, including the astronomical bill from last night's dinner. My watch. Three 20-franc coins. My cell phone was gone.

I stared at this still life for a moment as if I could will it into something else. A gun. A knife. Something more useful in my present circumstances. I took out an American Express card and dropped it on the floor, then carefully pushed it under the bottom of the electric heater beneath the window. If I was moved today, the card would be evidence of my presence here. I put my wallet and pen back in my pocket, leaving only a 20-franc piece on the windowsill.

With the coin firmly in hand, I set to work scraping at the tiny line in the white paint, over and over. The building faced east, this much I knew. The sun hit the painted windows full force, warming the room. In an hour, I had cleared an opening about the size of the coin. Sweat dripped down my neck. Particles swam among the beam of sunlight that came through this small opening, my useless work for the morning. Even if I cleared more paint, what could I do next? I had thought of writing a note for help and holding it up to the cleared patch. But who would see it? Peering through the circle confirmed that all of the other windows in the building were also painted white. The cement plaza behind the building looked abandoned, without bicycles, trash, or other evidence that anyone lived here. Factories and other buildings hovered in the smoky distance, miles away. I abandoned my scraping, carefully hiding the 20-franc piece above the window.

I walked back through the larger room to the sleeping room. On top of the carton waited two cardboard cylinders that hadn't been there before. I opened them cautiously. The first contained warm brown rice. The smaller held a steamed green, kale, I supposed. *Just my luck*, I thought. *To be held hostage by vegetarians.* I wondered how the food, such that it was, had appeared here so effortlessly.

There was a narrow door flush against the far wall of the bedroom, without a doorknob or exposed hinges. Placing my ear to the door, I could hear a telephone pulsing and people talking. It sounded more like an office than another apartment. I knocked on the door as hard as I could with my fist until it hurt but all I made was a muffled thump. When I shouted, my voice sounded ridiculous and so I gave up.

Back on the futon, I reached into the first cylinder and ate a pinch of the greens. They were bitter but still warm. A little garlic. Possibly sautéed in sesame oil. I reached into the other cylinder and took a handful of brown rice, plain but satisfying to someone who had eaten only an apple all morning. Not having a utensil of any type, I ate with my fingers, which were soon sticky with rice. When I was done, I replaced the lids and walked into the bathroom to wash my hands. The water was cold and I left my hands under it for several minutes, closing my eyes and imagining that I could swim into the tap and down through the building, emerging in the waterworks in Antwerp or Brussels. When I was a boy, I used to pretend I was a shrinking boy who could travel unnoticed along drainpipes and telephone wires.

When I came back into the bedroom, I saw a white plastic fork on top of the taller cylinder. I picked it up, then looked at the closed door. I was being watched, and carefully too. Someone was attending to my needs, though I wasn't sure who.

"How about a glass of wine?" I shouted. "Perhaps a white would be nice." I thought about a cold glass of Graves, bone dry to cut through the gluey rice. Or a manzanilla served ice cold. But there was no response. The door stayed closed.

I lay down on the futon and stared up at the ceiling. Aluminum ducts coursed through the entire apartment with grated openings every few feet. Through these came air, and, I suppose, cameras, microphones, and whatever else was being used to monitor me.

"So now what?" I asked the grate.

No answer.

"So you've kidnapped an American. You could have done better, you know. No one is going to pay a cent for my return. I'm unimportant." I spoke firmly, with conviction. "No one cares about me."

I wondered if anyone had even noticed that I was gone yet. My schedule was my own, and I very rarely went into the main office. I had already missed two meetings this morning and hoped that someone had called in, wondering where I was. Perhaps then I would be found missing. I thought of Alec Moore, the young chief at IBIS, so preoccupied with his meetings, his tedious presentations at The Hague with carefully tested statements supported by bulleted proof points. I was just a shadowy elder to him, a man from another generation, not particularly venerated.

Maura, my wife, wouldn't notice I was missing until our call at the end of the week. She was back on our farm, *holding down the fort,* as she put it. My schedule for the last few years—alternating months in Brussels and Washington—had disconnected us. Our time together had turned pleasant rather than passionate. After thirty years of marriage our passions were elsewhere. We didn't call each other every hour the way we had when we were just married. In fact, there were days when I hardly thought of her. Now though, I wanted her to call, to notice my absence. But I knew that Maura, always dependable, would call only Friday night as we planned, still days away.

I paced around the apartment. My thoughts turned inward, searching for a reason why I was here. Was it a chance that brought me here? Or had I been singled out? Perhaps the dinner was set up to trap me, keep me out late, dull me for capture without a struggle. I discarded this notion. I had worked with my dinner companions for years and they had all profited handsomely from our relationship—as I had. I doubted any complicity on their part.

IBIS. The name sounded so beautiful, summoning up a white bird standing gracefully among the everglades. In truth, our work was neither graceful nor beautiful. Over the years, the International Business Interest Sector had transformed from an obscure strategy group within the Commerce Department to an independent agency, a matchmaker among U.S. and European businesses. It certainly wasn't the sort of work I imagined doing for the rest of my life back when I graduated from college. But what was life but a series of carefully considered compromises? I had certainly made mine.

My life's work was remarkably unimportant, and I never did anything to raise anyone's hackles. After all, our mission was strictly commercial, not political. The staggering U.S. trade deficit was our only stated enemy, although I now recognize it as unconquerable, a glacier to our tiny ice axes. At the root of my work was the simple fact that too many incoming foreign goods and not enough exports do not make for a sustainable economy. Earlier in my time with IBIS, I was ardent about this growing inequity. I stood on the economic frontier, protecting the American worker. The matchmaking I did added up to millions of dollars in export contracts. I used to chart my results, confident that it made a difference. But I was merely a foot soldier in a European economic skirmish while the bigger battles raged in the Far East.

As usual, this career review left me sullen. I paced my bedroom, skirting the edges of the futon, and took a kick at the wall, which I found to be of solid, Belgian construction rather than American drywall. I put my ear to the door and heard the distant voices again, a couple of electronic beeps, phones perhaps. Who were they? Certainly none of the IBIS member corporations, U.S. or European, harbored any grudge against us. Ours was a game in which everyone won. In any case, it was only business. No software developer in Amsterdam or manufacturer of printing plates in Leverkusen was going to take offense at my work. Marginal incursions into their market share was hardly reason enough to resort to taking hostages.

Then again, perhaps this event was personal in nature. In this area, I had even less to worry about. As my work would suggest, I was sociable, hospitable, able to convince even the thickest, most provincial middle manager that I was his best friend. I was loyal to Maura, never straying in any way, not so much as a kiss. My personal life was remarkably without intrigue or duplicity.

I gave up searching for someone to blame for my present circumstances. They would show themselves shortly, no doubt. All would be revealed. I lay down to sleep—not the deep, unburdened sleep of the innocent, but the fitful sleep of the singled out, the guilty held without charge.

♪♪♪

Day 3. Today's insight—being detained is very boring. The day passed slowly. Hours of work at the window with the 20-franc coin, the press of my thumbnail in the plaster to mark the day, a few notes written and tucked into corners of my apartment, the stealthy arrival of food cartons—these events did little to speed the flow of the day. In the long dull afternoon, whatever fear I had dissipated. If they were going to chain me to a wall and beat me, they would have started already. They wouldn't be feeding me hot meals and keeping me in these relatively comfortable circumstances. I convinced myself that behind the seamless door, my captors had realized that they had grabbed the wrong man. Even Alec Moore, our feckless leader, wouldn't merit much attention or money.

I stayed in the bedroom most of the morning, hoping to catch sight of the invisible staff that spirited away my food after every meal and delivered more. If I left the room I laid a trap I thought clever, stacking three empty liter bottles against the door so they would topple over at the slightest motion.

That afternoon, I went into the larger room for exercise hour. I assumed that exercise was an important part of the hostage experience, a way of staying healthy and sane. Stripped down to my boxers, I ran in circles until my heart pounded and the room spun. Sweat poured down my face and the air tasted sour with dust. I drank some water *avec gaz*—the carton contained a mixture of still and sparkling, another sign that my captors were civilized. I did a few halfhearted push-ups. If my keepers were watching, certainly they would have pity on me. A life in Washington and Brussels did not make for health. A weekly jog, the occasional weekend with Maura at a spa in Maryland, the weekend chore around the farm that required lifting—these were my sporadic defenses against heavy cream, Bordeaux, and Dunhills.

I turned on my back and did a few sit-ups, *crunches*, as they were called, implying that there was something to crunch. With each sit-up, my soft stomach, usually hidden beneath a suit, revealed itself. I wondered when the sight of my own body had become so displeasing to me. The idea of being watched quickly brought my exercising to a close. I lay back on the floor and stared up at the aluminum ducts, wondering who was watching me now.

"A book!" I shouted. "And new clothes, I've been wearing this suit for three days for God's sake. And a carton of cigarettes. Dunhill's in the red pack. Those are my demands. For the moment." I gave a nervous laugh, hoping that my observers also had a sense of humor. Then I closed my eyes and waited for my heart to stop pounding from the run.

When I woke, the light filtering through the painted windows had paled. In the empty bedroom, the beam of sunlight from my scraped circle projected a tiny orange sun on the wall. I had been asleep for hours. I walked back into the bedroom to wash up. The usual cartons of food waited next to the futon. Stacked next to them were a pair of lightweight tan trousers, three pairs of underwear, and three white undershirts. I picked up the clothes and found that they were all my size and of German manufacture. On the other side of the futon was a red carton of Dunhill's and a stack of books. I picked each up, found that they were used, with slightly torn covers. The prices penciled inside were in Belgian francs. They were all relatively inexpensive, in English, and apparently randomly chosen—an illustrated book called *Ships of the World*, a faded travel guide to the Congo that focused on the bargains to be found at certain markets, a volume of Cosima Wagner's diary, and a book on metallurgy.

"Thanks," I said up to the grate above my bed. As a child, I personified certain places in my room—the chair next to the window was my mother, in the far corner dwelled friends from school. I was never alone, even at night. For now, the overhead grate was my overseer, audience, judge.

DAY 4. I settled into a routine that allowed me to convince myself that I had control, a comforting thought. In a way, I could do what I wanted, as long as it was within the confines of the empty apartment. Mornings I spent reading *Ships of the World*. Sailing was never of much interest to me, but now it all seemed fascinating. I read each paragraph carefully. The keel length of the Albans schooner. The route between New York and London that skirted the Grand Banks. I realized how little I knew about ships. I decided that once I was released, Maura and I would go on a cruise. For now, I did my best to forget that this apartment was not my own, that all the food, clothes, and even my books came from someone just beyond the door.

My thoughts escaped my prison though I couldn't. On weekends, Maura and I used to drive west from Washington through eastern Virginia, watching the city give way to towns, the towns give way to country roads. At some point near Tynsdale, we would stop the car and set out on foot. We carried only a small backpack with our lunch and some books to read. How simple and free that time seemed. It surfaced in my thoughts often during these early days—an antidote to the present.

It was during a weekend trip that Maura and I first walked the long lane past two barns and grazing fields gone to high grass, all boundaried by toppled stone walls. At the end of the lane we saw the tall, two-story house, vaguely Greek Revival in style, but made of pale stone carefully pieced together and topped with a slate mansard roof. Weeds poked from the mortar and the slate was missing patches like a half-scaled trout. Above the front door, we could see words carved in the stone. Triangle Farm, 1819. The odd house awed us at first sight. What had driven someone to build a house so sturdy and formal so far in the country? I envisioned a Jeffersonian in exile, perhaps a lesser politician who wanted to build an empire. Whatever motivation led to its birth was now lost to history, leaving behind only the ruins, which we explored for hours.

The idea occurred to us both slowly. We could buy the farm and restore it. We realized that we wanted to live in the country, not just visit it every weekend. It was 1980, the dawning of the awful Reagan years, a fine time to leave Washington. We were in our mid-thirties and our idealism was giving way to less palatable realities. My work consisted of writing economic policy papers that rarely found their way further than a dozen or so readers, none of whom were in any position to act on my recommendations. Besides, the economy was sputtering, a gilded engine with corroded works.

Maura worked at a small nonprofit agency that funded land conservation. The work that initially interested her had grown stale, and she was eager for distraction.

Our marriage, too, was at a quiet point. The slowing of desire leaves a void. Some have children. Others have affairs. For us, the farm was to become our preoccupation, our forty-acre ward. The initial excitement at its purchase gave way to the realization of the enormity of the work ahead, which would drain the rest of our savings and more.

While everyone else in Washington was having power lunches and darting about in limousines, we lived like ill-prepared pioneers. After months of hard work, the farm's original beauty emerged, a landscape freed from yellow varnish. Weekend visitors laughed at our album of "before" photos, amazed at the transformation. With some satisfaction, I charted our tax assessment as it doubled, tripled, and more. Maura's reward was less fiduciary. Triangle Farm gave her a purpose, a center to her life that she had not found before. It anchored her when I started traveling more, gave her an endless flow of responsibilities that she found rewarding, and made up for our less-than-perfect union. The name seemed prescient. Triangle Farm. The farm, Maura, and I formed a triangle as unlikely and solid as the farm's stone walls.

At midday, I became less convinced that I would be returning to the farm soon. The apartment hummed with a certain efficiency that hinted at permanence. It seemed set up for a long incarceration, perhaps months. I thought of the Iranian hostages back at the end of the Carter years. They were imprisoned for more than four hundred days. I remembered seeing the gaunt, bearded face of Terry Anderson staring from the cover of *The Washington Post* every now and then. As the years passed, he seemed almost an embarrassment, forgotten and lost somewhere in a Beirut cellar. Weeks in captivity, much less years, filled me with dread. I wanted my time as a hostage to be brief, a footnote, a story I could tell in meetings or after dinner.

My life of a few days ago was remarkably predictable. I might have to go to a meeting in Berlin on short notice. There were regular rumors that IBIS was shutting down or merging with another agency. Friends had heart attacks or surgery and Maura and I visited them in the hospital. Calls from Roanoke told me of great-aunts and great-uncles who had died in nursing homes. Colleagues called to announce their divorces. Cars crashed. People were injured and got better. The low, flat terrain of my life had lulled me into believing that nothing was ever going to happen to me.

Day 5. I carefully took apart my cardboard food cylinders and washed and dried them in the bathroom, the room least likely to be under surveillance. I scrawled a note—*My name is Eliott Gast. I am an American being held hostage in the upper floor of the building with white windows. Please help me.* I wrote the phone number of the IBIS office and my home number in Virginia. I repeated the same note on three different pieces of cardboard, which I hid in my back pocket.

Back in the main room, I picked up one of the metal chairs and walked quickly toward the painted windows. Raising the chair over my head, I smashed it as hard as I could into the glass. It rebounded, leaving only a small chip in the paint. I raised the chair high over my head and struck again and again, the crash of metal echoing through the apartment. Sweat coursed down my face. I retreated to the far end of the apartment and ran at the window, throwing the chair as hard as I could. The chair clattered to the floor. My plan to drop the notes from the broken window seemed foolish. I bent over and heaved, the air thick and sharp, my mind burning with frustration.

When I rose, I saw dozens of black cables had snaked out of the ducts and now waited, extended and watching, for me to continue.

"Damn you!" I jumped to grab a cable, but it had retracted into the ceiling again.

"I suggest you stop that immediately." A woman's voice came from somewhere.

"What?" My voice sounded strange after so much silence.

"The glass will not break. It is unnecessary for you to try."

"Where are you?" I demanded, looking up at the ceiling.

"You needn't shout," the voice said in accented English. "I'm in the next room."

I walked across the apartment and stopped at the door of the far bedroom. Seated in the remaining chair was a small woman in jeans, a white blouse, and a black-and-white head scarf that hid all of her face except her eyes. My thoughts raced. *Hezbollah. Algerian separatists. Fanatical Muslims.* I was in the hands of true terrorists, not just kidnappers. I tried to recall anyone that might have influence. I had met Queen Noor once at a reception. I knew a handful of Iranian businessmen in London.

"It is a costume, a disguise," the woman said, divining my thoughts from my worried look. She pointed to the ceiling.

"We're being watched?"

"Of course." She gestured to the windowsill and I sat down. I noticed that the small scraped opening I had been working on had been painted over, leaving the smell of resin.

She said nothing for a few moments and I waited. I suppose I expected a full explanation of why I was here to come bursting forth from her. I took a close look at the strip in the head covering that revealed deep brown eyes, the faint line of carefully shaped

21

eyebrows, the delicate bridge of her nose. Her eyes glistened and held a familiar glow that I soon placed. Maura used to read diaries and memoirs for distraction from more substantial books. The eyes of my captor reminded me of Anais Nin's dewy gaze on the cover of volume after volume of her diaries, looking for Henry Miller in a crowd of Frenchmen. And from that distant association came the name that I would call her.

"Why am I here?" I asked Nin.

She shrugged. "I am not here to speak of ideology. I am your liaison. Nothing more."

"Liaison to . . ."

"To the others. They make the plans."

I noted the separation between Nin and the others, hoped that it implied that she could be reasoned with. "And what are these plans?"

Again, she shrugged. "They will come about in time. For now, I am to check to make sure that your needs are met and that you are comfortable. Your accommodations, I assume, are pleasing to you?"

I nodded. "For a jail, yes, I suppose it's fine. But I am being detained illegally. I demand that I be released immediately."

She shook her head. "This is only the beginning. Undoubtedly, you are afraid. It is normal."

"My family will be very concerned. My wife will have alerted the authorities in the U.S., and my children will be . . ."

"You have no children," Nin stated flatly.

I paused, taken aback. "Who is in charge here? What do they want from me?"

"Again, your questions go beyond what I can answer." Her voice was quiet and engaging, as if we were exchanging pleasantries in a café. "Perhaps you need reassurance. Know this, then. We are committed to our ideals, but we are not extremists."

"The difference?"

"Extremists wear the bomb." Her eyes brightened at this definition, as if it were a witticism. "We don't even have a bomb. All we have is you."

"I'm flattered."

"Perhaps you should be." Nin shifted slightly forward and the metal chair rasped. "Your role is important. The most important of all."

"You make it sound like I'm part of whatever you have planned."

"Aren't you?"

"No. I was grabbed off the Rue du Marché four days ago."

Nin leaned forward. "Your arrival here was no accident."

I said nothing.

"We've been watching you for some time."

"For how long?"

"Since London."

Our operation moved from London to Brussels almost a decade ago. I shifted nervously in my seat. Nin stood up and walked toward me. She stood just a few inches over five feet. For a moment, I considered grabbing her and turning the tables. But it was just a passing thought. Heroics were beyond me.

"We will speak again, Monsieur Gast. In the meantime, all I can tell you is that most hostages live," she said with remarkable vagueness, then added a more cryptic note. "Unless they decide not to."

I laughed uncomfortably.

She moved closer and whispered. "This is no time for humor.

Something is about to happen to you, Monsieur Gast. Something that will change you forever. I advise you to prepare."

She turned and left the room. I stayed on the windowsill for a moment, then walked back through the apartment, the light fading. There was no trace of Nin. She had vanished beyond the walls to rejoin her invisible compatriots.

♪♪♪♪♪♪

DAY 6. Time passed extremely slowly, even more so knowing that I was being watched so closely. In any empty moment, Nin's words surfaced and sent a disturbing chill through me. *Something is about to happen to you.* Perhaps this declaration was the actual torture. Telling me that something was about to happen put me in a state of perpetual and uncomfortable anticipation. I stalked around the three rooms. Reading gave me little distraction. In the middle of the book on metallurgy, I slammed it closed and threw it across the room, disgusted with myself. I was not given to confrontation, but my questions had piled up until I could no longer get free of them without answers.

"What's going to happen?" I shouted up at the grate.

No answer.

"I demand that I be released."

Nothing.

I threw *Ships of the World* at the grate and it fell to the floor, pages splayed and fluttering like a pigeon on the cobblestones of the Grand-Place.

The afternoon was cloudy and the light filtering through the painted windows turned thin and pale. Gloom settled throughout the apartment. Maura would know something was wrong and would have contacted the embassy. I had faith in her thoroughness and resolve. She would set about the search that would trace me here to this apartment and set me free.

The lights came on one after the next, not because I needed them to see—I was through with metallurgy and ships of the world for today. They came on because they needed to observe me, their prisoner, their pet.

I imagined Nin's dark eyes taking in my unshaven face, my rumpled clothes. Perhaps she regretted telling me anything. She could have let me think that nothing was going to happen, that I was just an innocent bystander. But I knew this wasn't the case.

DAY 7. A burning smell woke me. I looked over at the windowsill, where I kept my ashtray and cigarettes. Leaning on the windowsill was a man wearing a plastic pirate mask with a black patch over one eye. At the top of the mask perched a jaunty three-pointed buccaneer hat bearing a skull and crossbones. The bottom of his mask ended in a black plastic beard, followed by several inches of his own sleek, black beard. I could see dark eyes peering through small holes in the mask.

Blackbeard smoked by holding the cigarette carefully in the mouth hole of the mask. When he exhaled, the smoke spouted from the mask's nose.

"You have good taste." He pointed to the Dunhill's with the cigarette he had taken.

I sat up and got out of bed, pulling my trousers on, then my shoes. By the time I was dressed, Blackbeard had lit another cigarette and offered it to me. His hands were callused and his thick, earthy fingers ended in closely cropped nails. I took the cigarette and retreated to the corner of the room, where I sat on the carton of bottled water.

"I've heard that you are concerned." With his accent, the first two words sounded like *I've hurt.* He was German, Flemish, Dutch. I couldn't tell.

"I'm concerned that I'm being held here against my will for almost a week now," I said. "And I demand to be released."

Blackbeard waved his hand in front of him. "In good time, Eliott Gast. In the meantime, don't think of it as being detained."

"Really?"

"No. You are being punished."

"For *what?*"

"Your sins. Just as everyone is punished for theirs."

"And what exactly are those sins?"

"You know what they are."

"No, I don't."

He paused, flicked ashes on the floor. "Your work offends us a great deal."

"I'm sorry to hear that." I looked away, and in that moment, Blackbeard left the windowsill and moved quickly toward me. He grabbed my shirt and threw me to the floor, then kicked me in the stomach. I fell on the floor, stunned, my hands pressing on my stomach. The blow was not particularly hard, but it surprised me. I listened to the wheezing of my fast breathing.

Blackbeard leaned toward me. He smelled of cigarettes and coffee. "I insist that we speak directly, without any of your American insolence. Truly, it will do you no good here."

I dusted myself off. The hollow ache in my stomach faded. Blackbeard returned to his windowsill and picked up the cigarette he had carefully balanced on its filter.

I stood. "I am not a spy."

"Yes, we know that." His voice was deep and smooth, an actor's voice. "You are worse."

"I am an economist."

"Then describe your work to me."

"I promote international collaboration and trade."

"For . . . ?"

"For corporations, mostly in the U.S. But any group interested in expanding foreign trade can join IBIS."

"IBIS." Blackbeard laughed. "IBIS is your country's economic CIA."

I shook my head. "Our work has nothing to do with politics."

"It has everything to do with politics. You know this, Gast. You make it sound like you are some kind of . . . of clerk writing numbers in a ledger all day. Your work, as you know, has much wider impact. You have directly contributed to economic globalization."

"Perhaps we've affected the balance of trade a bit," I offered. "But I can't say that it goes any further than that."

"Then you are being modest, as well as lying."

"Of what possible concern is my work to you?" I asked finally. "And what have I done to deserve this?" I pointed at the room.

Blackbeard paced in front of me much like a middle manager about to draw a chart. Then he turned back to me, eyes glinting behind his mask.

"You asked about our ideology. Perhaps this will help you understand, at least as much as you need to understand. Let's start at the very beginning. Think back to the time of the initial talks about a European union. Recall that there were demonstrations throughout Europe."

"Yes." I remembered a certain amount of dissent from the usual groups—nationalists on one extreme, ultra-left groups on the other, anarchists everywhere. The newspapers had covered the protests.

"We failed to gain attention for our cause at that crucial juncture," Blackbeard said. "And much of the blame goes to you and your group, the so-called IBIS, which steamrolled all of Europe into this farcical union."

I shook my head. "I had absolutely nothing to do with that." I almost laughed at the thought. "Unification had been coming for decades. Since the Treaties of Rome in 1957."

"But accelerated by you and your friends. You can tell yourself what you want to, but your role is clear to us, and well documented."

"As far as I know, the motivation came from Europe, not from the U.S.," I offered.

"But your financial incentives greased the wheels. And they laid the groundwork for globalization, didn't they, Eliott Gast?"

I shrugged. "I have no idea what you're talking about." I wondered if Blackbeard had me confused with another, more highly placed American diplomat.

Blackbeard paced again. "Audio on," he shouted up at the ceiling, then spoke again, louder this time. "The European Economic Community is an American ploy. What better way to weaken us than to join us together—like a marriage of cousins. It was invented by scheming Americans concerned about their own agenda—keeping foreign markets open, cultural domination, and the expansion of the American empire. Remember your history, Eliott Gast. They must have taught you this at Princeton. America today is like England of Victoria. Except that its empire is hidden. Its battles do not take place on open seas, but in the boardrooms of the World Bank, the G8, the World Trade Organization, and your beloved corporations. Transfer of power does not take place on a battlefield, but via movement of enormous sums of money."

He stopped for a moment. "Here is the source of our anger. Once we are dominated economically, it will not be long until we are absorbed financially, culturally, and militarily. We are fighting to break up the union and return power to the individual countries that formed it. To do this, we are exposing the American economic conspiracy. In short, we are making an example of you."

"I think you could have chosen a better representative of American imperialism."

"Audio off," Blackbeard shouted up at the ceiling. Then he turned to me. "That, like so many other things, is not up to you to decide. You have made your own choices, your own decisions about what you have done with your life, and now you must be willing to accept the consequences."

"Whatever your opinion of me, my work, or my government, one thing is certainly clear. I am being held here illegally." I spoke carefully. "You must release me immediately. Certainly it does your cause no good to take hostages."

"On that point, you are wrong, Gast. Capturing you is the best thing that's ever happened to us. You are like the golden goose to us. The one that lays the golden eggs." Blackbeard's eyes crinkled behind the mask. "We will talk again. I enjoyed our discussion."

I didn't bother pointing out that there was no discussion, merely a lecture. Blackbeard's position was laughable—a mix of conspiracy theory, tired anti-Americanism, and globalization mumbo-jumbo. But I found his commitment frightening. He was clearly a man who had developed an elaborate and misguided theory, one where I was being cast as a villain. Nin was wrong. They were extremists.

"For now, get some sleep. Tomorrow is a very important day. A very important day." Blackbeard stubbed out his cigarette suddenly and strode from the room, as if he remembered an appointment elsewhere. I sat on the cardboard carton and wondered how I could possibly convince this group, whatever it was called, that they had the wrong man.

DAY 8. When confronted with danger, animals pretend to ignore it and blend into their surroundings. A rabbit may look the other way and hold stock still until a cat is out of distance. An opossum might pretend to be dead. This survival technique for the animal world was known as *Batesian mimicry*. I had learned about it in biology class back in Roanoke and hadn't thought about it since. But what could I do to elude them? The apartment seemed more like a prison. The group's intent was still not clear, but it was far from innocent. Blackbeard's rant still echoed in the room, his anger amplifying. All I could do was ignore it, the way fearful animals do. Instead, I went about my hostage business as well as I could. I awoke, ate my cereal, brushed my teeth, read a chapter on extracting iron ore from taconite. But all the while, I braced myself for their return.

Late in the afternoon, they rushed into the room while I was chipping away with my 20-franc coin. By the time I turned, three people stood before me—Nin, Blackbeard, and a man I hadn't seen before, thin, wearing a long white lab coat. He wore a simple black Zorro mask over his eyes, one that did little to disguise him.

"Showtime, Eliott Gast." Blackbeard pointed to the metal chair. I sat down and the metal legs squealed. The lights went up to full force and the black cables lowered slowly from every grate in the room. My heart started to pound.

"I've explained your role." Blackbeard squatted in front of me. "Now it's time for you to do your part."

I nodded to the ludicrous pirate, not sure what he meant. Behind him, Nin stood holding a large metal bowl, the kind used for mixing greens. If there was any emotion in her eyes I could not detect it. They held only the same glinting darkness that I had seen during her first visit.

Behind her, the thin doctor rushed around, white coat flapping. He hunched slightly in the way that children who grow too tall learn to reduce themselves. His skin was tanned, hair black and thin, bald on the top. He could be Basque, Arab, Algerian. It was not clear at all. Perhaps this was the reason why he had such a perfunctory disguise. He was not particularly recognizable.

He seemed to be looking for something along the baseboards of the apartment. Near the windows, he found an electrical outlet. Then he reached into his black bag and took out an iron, a simple steel iron with its familiar chevron of holes for steam, a turquoise plastic handle, and a long cord, which he plugged into the wall.

The iron was an ordinary item found in any home, similar, in fact, to the one Maura and I had at home. Still, in this context it became freighted with a new meaning. We all watched the iron as it sat on the windowsill, clicking as it warmed. After a moment, the Doctor reached over and touched the surface with his fingertip, then turned the heat up to the highest setting.

Nin tapped her fingers on the metal bowl, sending a small ringing through the room. Blackbeard reached out and grabbed her wrist, jerking his head up at the grates. She stopped.

In a few more moments, the Doctor tested the iron again and found it to his liking. He nodded to Blackbeard.

Blackbeard shifted behind my chair and leaned his face close to mine. I could feel his beard bristling against my face. "Let's begin, shall we?"

I nodded involuntarily, not knowing what was beginning. Sweat coursed down my sides and my breathing turned shallow.

The Doctor reached into his black bag and took out a syringe, which he carefully filled with a clear fluid from a small vial.

He held it toward me as if offering me a piece of fruit or a cigarette, eyebrows raised.

I shook my head, not sure what was in the syringe, but certain that it could do me no good.

"I suggest you accept this injection gratefully," Blackbeard whispered. "It's merely a painkiller, intended to help you. Be thankful we're not amateurs." He reached over my shoulders and grasped the arms of the chair, effectively pinning me. I struggled but could only flail my legs. I'm sure I was shouting the entire time, involuntarily yelling *no, stop it, let me go* and the like. But I was deaf to my own words. I heard only a roaring in my ears.

I kept kicking until the Doctor reached into his bag and removed two lengths of rubber ending in metal clips. We used similar cords to secure our canoe to the roof of the car back at the farm. *Bungee cords.* The words sounded strange and ridiculous to me. Although I struggled, the Doctor quickly secured my ankles tightly to the legs of the chair. I could only try to lunge forward, which did little except to encourage Blackbeard to hold my shoulders even more firmly against the back of the chair. The needle stung my forearm, then a slow warming moved up my arm.

Looking straight ahead, I saw the Doctor approaching, a half-smile frozen on his tight face. In his right hand, he held a set of metal tongs with tan rubberized handles, the kind used in the kitchen to move pasta from a pot or to gather up asparagus. We had exactly the same tongs in our kitchen. But seeing such a familiar object gave me no comfort. The Doctor opened the tongs and reached toward me. I shouted again, and with that shout he grasped the tip of my tongue. The metal cinched together and I couldn't get loose. He pulled so firmly that I thought for a moment he intended to rip my tongue out of my mouth. My mind raced despite the injection.

Nin moved closer, kneeling and holding the bowl beneath my chin, as if in a ritual. Her eyes darted from my face to the bowl to the Doctor.

I watched her eyes widen suddenly and realized that the Doctor held a long fillet knife in his right hand. With his left, he gave one last pull, so the pain at the base of my tongue was almost intolerable. Then he flicked the knife forward suddenly, like a waiter opening a trout. In that moment, the pain blossomed a thousand-fold. The entire length of my tongue blazed. He took a step away and I could see that the tongs held a thin layer of flesh curling one way and then the other like an eel. He dropped it in the bowl and I heard it ring. I screamed. Blood splattered along the metal. Nin deftly moved the bowl to catch it. I could feel my tongue slipping against my lips as I screamed again.

"Almost over," Blackbeard shouted. He tightened his grasp firmly and I saw the Doctor coming at me with the tongs again in his right hand, the iron in his left, its cord trailing behind. In the eye-holes of his mask, I detected no particular expression. It was as if he were simply completing a task he had been assigned and doing it as efficiently as he could.

He reached out suddenly with the tongs and managed to grasp my tongue again, this time holding it by the sides. I felt Blackbeard's hand on my jaw, holding it down. The painkiller had entered my system, making me feel a strange detachment from the scene, as if I floated up to the ceiling among the grates and black cables. I envisioned myself pinned in my chair, fearful and unwilling. At my feet, Nin held the ringing bowl like a chalice. Blackbeard's firm embrace seemed almost brotherly. And the impassive Doctor seemed to be searching for the correct way to bring about a cure to my bleeding. Together, we created a perverse medieval still life. The Curing of the Damaged.

The Doctor brought the iron close to my mouth and it seared my tongue, sending the flames of pain rising again. Smoke drifted past my eyes and I smelled meat cooking on a grill. He pressed the iron down firmly for a moment and my eyes closed against all that was happening here in an unidentified apartment somewhere in Belgium, in the middle of a long fall afternoon. I left the white room and traveled back to the farm, to walk along the trails through the deep woods, the maple leaves thick along the path, all pain gone from the world.

♪ ♪ ♪ ♪♪ ♪ ♪ ♪

DAY 9. Now that I would never taste wine again, I spent the morning huddled beneath a blanket, remembering the particular flavor of Bordeaux. Each bottle fixes time at the summer harvest, growing more complex with each passing year. I always thought of drinking wine as a way to recapture summer in winter, to travel back to the past without leaving the dinner table.

At a quiet restaurant in Kensington, Maura and I had a 1945 Chateau Margaux to celebrate our last night in London. We had to convince the waiter that we wanted this particular bottle, that we were aware of the price. It was once one of the world's finest wines. His hands shook as he opened the bottle and poured a tiny portion into my glass. The wine had been in its bottle for almost fifty years, a time capsule from another era. The harvest almost forgotten until late August, when the grapes were overripe and bursting, as if the vines were celebrating victory as well. From my first sip I could taste the wine coming unraveled, the flavors drifting apart with age. It was a wine with pathos, my favorite. A dark, smoky flavor of sugar left too long in a cast iron skillet gave way to the smooth, empty middle of the wine, pleasant where it had once been thrilling. The finish stung my mouth for a moment, then dropped off.

The wine took me back to my father's dark study, lined with faded novels and smelling of cherry pipe tobacco, where he and my mother had danced when they heard the war was over. I imagined sitting on the floor and watching them, hearing Darby fire his cap pistol over and over out on the lawn. The rush of nostalgia overwhelmed me for a moment in the restaurant, bringing tears to my eyes. Maura watched me curiously and the waiter asked whether perhaps the wine was past its prime. I promised him it was very fine.

I longed to disappear into the past again for a few moments, but I was locked into the aftermath of yesterday's brutal operation. Without distraction, the pain pierced me. I had suffered only ordinary, minor injuries in my life. A compressed vertebra made my right arm tingle for a month. A cut on my hand from the gardening shears took five stitches to close. I bumped my head on the windshield when a delivery van ran into my Volvo one morning along the Beltway. The burning along the top of my tongue was beyond all of these. Wrapped now in gauze, my diminished tongue rested like a silenced bell clapper. Any movement set off the pain again. Nin, who sat cross-legged beside the futon, had helped me swallow two codeine tablets. They seemed only to free my mind, which could wander to Virginia or London. My body stayed here, trapped.

I could taste nothing. Perhaps there was a procedure that could reverse the work of the Doctor. It seemed unlikely. Rising out of my mouth came the inescapable sour smell. Only by rounding my lips and breathing carefully could I send it wafting away from me. The midmorning light filtering through the white windows was gentle and left no shadows. But the apartment had become soaked with pain the way a battle forever changes a grassy field. In one quick assault, everything was horribly changed. Nin, Blackbeard, and the Doctor were worse than jailers. They were no longer political activists with an extreme ideology. They were torturers.

More codeine. I scrawled on the black notebook Nin had given me. The bandages and the pain in my mouth left me able only to make noises. The extra pain of trying to speak was not worth the effort.

Nin took the black book and read the note. She checked her watch, a child's digital with a pink face. "Too soon. Fifteen minutes," she said softly. Nin put the black book on my lap, then leaned back. She sat motionless next to the futon. At times this morning I forgot she was in the room.

The black book was filling up with questions, demands, denunciations—all received by Nin with equal detachment. In her eyes, half-hidden by her scarf, I tried to detect some evidence that she was capable of doing something so brutal. Earlier, when the Doctor came in to check my bandages, I had recoiled into the corner of the room. But behind his mask, I could see in his eyes that he had come to help, that he intended no further damage, at least during this visit. So I moved closer, allowed him to reach into my mouth, where he had caused so much pain yesterday with one swift stroke of the knife. Perhaps he would take pity when he saw his terrible work. I thought of dogs, beaten but still returning. My urge to trust seemed to win out over the need to fear.

I could still picture Nin kneeling to hold the steel bowl beneath my chin, a supplicant catching blood. I looked at her dark eyes, centered in the narrow band above the scarf. How ordinary they were. Her eyes were not a window on her soul, but a veil to it. No intention could be found there. The faces of murderers, guards from death camps, boys who sprayed bullets across their playground—all were invariably unremarkable. Why was this such a surprise? If those who committed evil actually *looked* evil it would be too simple to single them out. The true measure of a person lay in what one actually did, not what one appeared capable of.

My mind wandered, retraced the coincidences that brought me here. I thought of this path as a white thread, fragile and innocent, knotted like a rosary. Following the white thread brought me to a spring afternoon, decades ago, when I was a senior at Princeton. Religious sunlight fell in a grid through the lead-paned windows of a cramped McCosh Hall office. My thesis advisor sat at his cluttered desk. At that time, he was an assistant professor of economics, a likable man with unruly dark hair and early jowls. Even then, he seemed to have great ambition, proven out years later, when he would join the Ford administration. On this May afternoon, we sat discussing my thesis, a serviceable exploration of the economic conditions that led to the French revolution. My point was that while others might view the revolution from political and social angles, economics was the real driving force behind this and so many other turning points of the eighteenth century— a point so obvious that it hardly needed two hundred pages to establish and prove. To read through my manuscript today would reveal the confidence of an innocent, the black-and-white judgments of an Aristotelian by default, unaware that the world was gray.

Outside, Cannon Green was quiet. The protesters had taken their bullhorns and signs home. Those who remained were apolitical, foreign, or committed more to academics than politics. The library stacks were filled with scholarly hiders who had burrowed into the endless floors of books while the ROTC building burned. I stayed because I found it laughable to think that by not completing school somehow the war in Vietnam would end. Besides, my father had made it clear that if I didn't finish college, he would personally ensure that I spent the rest of my days as a junior clerk at his insurance agency.

After we discussed my work, my advisor moved closer to speak softly to me, though the room was empty. "Wouldn't you like to do something more for your country than this?" He held up my thick manuscript. His gaze drilled intently at me. I paused for a moment. We had spent many office hours together and come to know each other well. But my advisor had misjudged me. I was not patriotic in any particular way, though I wasn't unpatriotic either. My continued presence on campus was more due to fear of my father than love of my country. But unwilling to offend, I nodded. Yes, I would like to do something more for my country. With that nod, a world opened to me that opens to few others.

Princeton's motto—*In the nation's service*—was intended to convey to its undergraduates a sense of duty to the larger world. Like those who came before us, we would do selfless service in the public sector, or as fair-minded attorneys or crusading journalists. Some graduates went on to make their mark in the public arena—Woodrow Wilson, F. Scott Fitzgerald, John Foster Dulles—all likeable and honorable to various degrees. On a more covert level, Princeton had always been a fertile recruiting ground for invisible functionaries. They entered the hidden layers of government, joining agencies with missions unknown to most Americans, to most politicians even. My advisor began an induction that, as he put it, "might lead to greater opportunities on the international front." My thesis topic, he assumed, indicated an interest in international affairs, an area where there were many avenues to explore. Eastern

Europe. Cuba. The Soviet Union. For now, I was to apply to the Foreign Language Institute in Monterey, California, ostensibly to take classes. There I would receive further instructions.

At the end of our final hour together, I thanked my advisor, because at that point foreign languages seemed far more interesting than actuarial tables. I left McCosh and walked down the flagstone path carpeted with bruised, perfumed flowers of tulip trees. In a haze, I drifted past stuffy Whig and Clio Halls, skirted the reddish prow of Edwards Hall, and returned to Cuyler, the drafty gothic keep where I had shivered all winter as I wrote my thesis. I stood outside the courtyard for a moment and watched the sun lowering slowly over the empty playing fields, too perfect and beautiful to be real. I had been given my first glimpse into an elaborate machine, one that was slowly pulling me in. This unasked-for insight made the world seem staged and false, a cover for the real workings that lay hidden deep inside.

Few people know what they want, or what is good for them. Only in retrospect do choices reveal themselves as right or wrong. On that auspicious day, only serendipity guided me. I was pretending to make choices that had been already been made by others. Doors were opening for me, phone calls being placed. Like a blind man, I walked holding my white thread, unsure of where it would lead but unwilling to let go.

I spent a year in Monterey, where my aptitude for languages and foreign service proved fatally low. I failed to exhibit the right characteristics, whatever they might be, that would have made me a better candidate for an illustrious career as a spy. I was given to introspection rather than observation. While my cohorts seemed to revel in the boot-camp regimen, I went to great lengths to avoid it. I was too bookish to be James Bond, not glib or ambitious enough to be an embassy chief.

But the white thread led me on in its own haphazard, innocent way. My senior year, I had met a young woman named Maura Emory, one of the first women at Princeton, the object of much attention from the newspapers and outrage from alumni. We stayed in touch when she came west to take graduate courses at Stanford. We spent our weekends driving down the coastal highway in her Corvair convertible, stopping in somber little restaurants in North Beach, the walls plastered with manifestos about the war. That fall, the last of the 1960s, we married and moved to Washington, a move that brought me one step closer to my Belgian prison.

"Eliott Gast."

I turned to Nin.

"You may take your tablet now." She handed me the codeine, the number 3 incised on its white surface.

When I stood, I felt unstable, a small boat in heavy seas. The combination of pain and painkillers, fear and boredom, left me numb, a neutral value charted along the day's wavering axis. I walked across the apartment to the bathroom, dragging my feet the whole way. In the mirror, I stared into my bloodshot eyes, saw the offending bandage, white tinged with reddish brown, lolling in my mouth like a gag. Taking medicine required that I push a pill past the bandage to the back of my throat. I got the pill in the right place, but suddenly found that I had no glass of water nearby. I turned on the tap, filled my hands, and carefully sipped the water to the side of my mouth, avoiding the bandage. By this time the tablet had adhered to my throat. I coughed but it didn't move. I coughed again, then choked. Unable to move my tongue, I could do little else. I fell to the floor and felt panic run through me like electricity. Curled on my side, I retched up the little portion of watery rice that I had managed to spoon past my bandage this morning. Among it lay the white pill, dissolving now. I picked it out and put it back in my mouth, waiting for bitterness, but tasting nothing.

Rolling on my back, I saw the black cables just inches away, retracting quickly as I swiped at them with my arm. "G'way," I mumbled.

They stayed at the edge of the duct, watching.

♪ ♪♪♪ ♪♪♪♪♪

DAY 10. Blackbeard squatted down next to my futon, his mask close to my face, his booming voice waking me. " . . . was absolutely brilliant, Gast. The bit with the pill. The sympathy is pouring in . . . and the money too, of course."

Had he negotiated a deal with IBIS for my return? For a moment I felt an uplift of hope. My captors had what they wanted and I would soon be released. I sat up slowly, one palm on the futon to steady myself.

Blackbeard waved his cigarette over a stack of papers. "Of course, it's not enough. Not even close to our stated goal."

I lay back down.

"Think of this unfortunate . . . injury, as a great opportunity," Blackbeard paced the room. "You Americans are always too hungry. Always eating. Eating as you work, as you walk. Devouring meat that your body is unable to digest. The fibres lodge and decay in the colon. It sickens me."

Blackbeard stopped to shudder for a moment, then went on with his pacing, his ranting. "Your leaders . . . your true leaders, the American corporate elite . . . simply want to buy and sell and fuck and eat." His hands whirled around him, pantomiming a hydra gathering all that was near and bringing it to its mouth. "Ideally, all would happen at once. In this convergence they would find true happiness." His neck reddened. "They are like bank accounts with fat bellies, small cocks, and art collections."

"Why are you doing this to me?" My voice was small, pathetic.

Blackbeard stopped pacing for a moment and looked at me, his piercing eyes burning from behind his mask.

"We want to present something new. No one has ever done what we are doing before, as far as we know."

"Done what? Torture?" The muffled words clung to the back of my mouth. "That's been done before."

Blackbeard paced again. "To truly change a man, you must take away what is most important to him. You must take a rich man's fortune. You must take a passionate man's wife. You are a man of the senses, Eliott Gast. So we are eliminating them. By this method we can leave you thoroughly changed. Through your example, we can change thousands."

I said nothing, stunned.

Blackbeard tugged at his plastic beard and let the elastic pull it back up. "Your nurse tells me the pain is getting better." He seemed to have forgotten that he was to blame for my present condition. Blackbeard took one of my cigarettes and held it out to me, then noticed the bloody bandage in my mouth and thought better of the offer.

He leaned against the doorframe. "Don't worry, Eliott Gast. We've captured their attention, and now we're working on getting our message across. So just rest. Relax. Gather your energy. We have much more collaboration to do, Gast. Much more."

Blackbeard left. I noticed that one of the papers from the stack had fluttered to the ground. Sitting up on the futon, I pulled aside the blanket and walked shakily over to the doorway. The page held two long columns of numbers, nothing more, reminding me of the reports that often crossed my desk at IBIS. They appeared to be dollar amounts, none particularly large. I wadded up the paper and tossed it toward the painted windows, glowing white from the afternoon sun.

It was true—the pain was better today. I could move my head without the unbearable stabbing that seemed to go all the way through to the back of my eyes. I could even move my bandaged tongue a little. My mind was groggy from the codeine. I was weak and hadn't eaten. But I was recovering. With little effort of my own, my body was mending the damage that the captors had done. The body was always optimistic, rallying again and again until the rallies stopped. It occurred to me that we survived all days but one, and this day, already at its midpoint, didn't seem fated as my last. I walked into the bathroom to shower away the sweat of fear and pain and begin again.

DAY 11. Dinner was a kind of rice soup, thinner than the usual fare. I used a long plastic teaspoon to carefully spoon the soup past my bandaged tongue and swallow it without too much pain. The soup was plain and unspiced, but whatever I ate had no taste, no sensation at all except that it was warm or cold going down my throat. Blackbeard was right about one thing—I was a man of the senses. For years, I had refined my palate with dishes that few have the pleasure to enjoy. Maura and I explored new cuisines, and cooking together was one of our great passions. We sought out

Burmese restaurants in New York, seafood shacks on the Maryland coast, pico roca downtown at La Fontaine. We wanted to taste everything.

A few years ago, the French economic officer and his wife hosted a weekend retreat at the Inn at Fox Creek, a luxurious hotel about an hour outside of Washington. It was billed as an opportunity to discuss our mutual economic concerns, but in fact it was designed to let us all spend a weekend eating and drinking like Romans. Our host had arranged for the kitchen to prepare the traditional southwestern French dish of ortolan. For years, Maura and I had heard of these tiny birds, a type of bunting. Captured alive, they were force-fed grains steeped in butter, then drowned in Armagnac. They were then roasted whole and eaten, bones and all, with the fingers. As each of the dozen dinner guests raised their glasses, our host gave a toast praising the continuation of traditions at all costs, which must have been significant, ortolan being extremely rare. The waiters then draped each of us with a large linen napkin, explaining that these would capture the precious scent of the roasted birds.

"Or hide your face from God," our host joked. I looked closely at the tiny bird in my hand, roasted to a golden finish. Dipping the ortolan into a brandy butter reduction, I raised it and saw suddenly the darkened eye of the bird, no bigger than a tiny bead, glistening now with a tear of butter. I paused, then gathered my resolve and took a first bite. The flesh was delicately flavored, slightly racy from the Armagnac and rich from the butter. But the real difference between ortolan and other game birds was the crunch of the tiny bones, thinner than matchsticks, then the final reward of the forest of roasted sweetmeats within. I spooned on more sauce and finished the bird in an uncontrollable swoon.

Around the table, the others hunched over their plates, shrouded by white linen. Behind each, a waiter stood by quietly to adjust each of our napkins, to refill our glasses with a golden Coteaux du Layon. Each face wore an expression of concentrated bliss, as if we each studied the beauty of the world through a microscope. In all, I ate six ortolans, but I could have eaten thirty given the chance.

To hide from God.

Perhaps I was paying now for my various excesses, for all I had done and left undone. I spooned rice porridge down my throat, though it might as well have been wallpaper paste for all I knew. Though I took no pleasure in this meal, it nourished me and stopped the shakiness in my legs. Perversely, I wondered what had become of the sliver of tongue that had been filleted away. Did it find its way to the public like young Getty's ear? Perhaps Alec Moore received it along with his morning mail, a raw and primitive message among the arcane financial data. Or had it just been tossed out with the rest of the papers, cigarette butts, empty food canisters, water bottles, and other refuse generated by this perverse community of myself, Nin, Blackbeard, the Doctor, and the unseen others beyond the apartment walls. To these questions and so many others, I had no answers.

I stared up at the grate on the ceiling and saw nothing, though I was surely being watched. "I want to leave, now!" I shouted at the grate, then began crying uncontrollably, tears of frustration and exhaustion. What had happened so far was terrible enough.

DAY 12. After dinner, I shaved with the disposable razor I found waiting at my sink. Gray and black stubble clung to the sink and I splashed water to send it on its way, then laughed at this habit. No one cared what I looked like, how neat I was, how I kept my prison cell. But my father taught me to keep up appearances, to do my chores without complaint.

In the mirror, my eyes were bloodshot and the skin on my forehead was taut and white. I reached into my mouth and began to unwrap the remaining gauze, carefully separating and unwinding it. The final layer stuck to the surface, and I dripped water from my fingertips to free it. I dropped the bandage into the trash, then turned to look for the first time at the damage. The blackened surface of my tongue was lined with glistening pink cracks. Dried blood crusted the edges. I spat the darkened bits into the sink. I spoke, careful not to move my tongue quickly or curl it in a way that would start more bleeding.

"I am Eliott Gast." The words whistled a little, but they were still recognizable. I could still speak, and in this I found a certain consolation.

I closed my mouth and looked at myself in the mirror. I was thinner perhaps by five pounds or more, but still recognizable. But then I opened my mouth and stuck out my tongue slowly, revealing myself as a damaged man, hideously so, forever changed. I shuddered and left the bathroom.

Nin waited in my room, perched on the edge of the chair next to my futon. I used to welcome her visits as a chance to talk. Not anymore. When I saw her, face hidden behind her checkered scarf, I could only picture her holding the bowl before her, catching my blood in its ringing center. Her gentle eyes were deceptive, simply part of her disguise.

"You are feeling better?"

I said nothing. I walked to the windowsill and stood looking out at the blank whiteness of another afternoon. I lived among the clouds here, each day flowing from darkness to gray to white to gray to darkness.

49

"I understand. It must hurt you to speak."

"You understand nothing," I said softly, my hardened tongue whistling.

"What do you mean?"

"If you really understood, you wouldn't allow them to continue."

Nin was quiet for a minute. "Audio off," she shouted.

No one responded.

"Audio off."

A click, then the disembodied voice muttered *oui*. Another click.

"I must speak quickly," she said. "While I believe in our goals, I do not approve of their methods. I said this from the start but was outnumbered. They are very enthusiastic, very persuasive. My voice was not heard among the others. When I question what is happening, they remind me that the only way to eliminate doubt is to eliminate the doubters. So I must keep my opinions to myself."

"A lot of good that does me," I said.

"I will help you, Eliott Gast. Believe me. Think of me as the jailer who will hand you the keys."

"Then hand them to me."

"In good time." Her eyes darted toward the doorway, where Blackbeard appeared, mask askew, an actor suddenly summoned onstage.

"What's going on?" he shouted. "I asked that the audio remain on at all times unless I say so."

"We were discussing his medical condition," Nin said. "And Monsieur Gast asked that we keep our discussion private."

"Private?" Blackbeard began to laugh, hands on his knees.

Nin looked away.

"I just want a few moments of privacy," I said.

"Let me explain," Blackbeard said when he had recovered. "It is not monitoring going on, like a camera in a bank. We are not just watching you, Eliott Gast. We are broadcasting you to the world every moment of the day and night. There can be no dead air."

The black snakes emerged from the ducts.

"Different views. Many angles. Audio. Video. Anyone can watch you right from their computer. What we are doing is like a TV show. You are like a celebrity . . . the first online hostage."

The black snakes retracted.

The idea sickened me it was so ingenious and perverse. Someone at their computer could watch me for a moment, then click over to check the weather or stock portfolio.

"Why? Why not just send photos to the newspaper?"

Blackbeard shook his head. "How twentieth century! Technology is the great enabler of radical causes. The Internet. Streaming video. Realtime transmissions. An archive of documents outlining our position. We have preserved every moment since you arrived. The incident with your tongue has proved remarkably popular." He thought for a moment. "Millions have downloaded it."

"Why are you doing this?" I yelled.

"Sustained interest in you generates more financial contributions for us. It is that simple."

Unlike Nin, Blackbeard seemed to have absolutely no second thoughts about what they were doing. It was as if he were outlining a business plan.

He turned to Nin. "In the future, all conversations must be recorded, understand?"

She nodded, her fingers spinning the tassels of her scarf.

Blackbeard left, with Nin following.

Alone in my room, I sat on the futon and lay back to stare at the ceiling. From one of the ducts, a black snake emerged and hovered

51

for a moment before retracting. These interlopers connected me to the world. They gave people a window on my prison, and they had flocked to it like voyeurs to a women's dorm. The advent of the first online hostage seemed as inevitable as it did evil.

Most hostages waited in obscurity, shuttled around miserable rooms in Beirut or Teheran. If they were held for long, their stories faded from the newspapers, with updates only on the anniversaries of their capture. But I was being held hostage in public, visible but hidden. Anyone who wanted to could watch me eat my rice, piss in the toilet, sleep. If they were lucky enough to watch at the right time, they might get to see me tortured, to witness my face twist with pain and fear as the Doctor wielded his knife. If they missed it, they could always watch later. How convenient—torture on demand. Our audience was waiting to see what would happen next, an ongoing program.

Though I hated knowing that my every moment was so public, it consoled me somehow to know that I was not alone. When I peered into the glinting end of one of the black snakes, perhaps Maura watched at the other end, her face lit by the computer screen, her hand reaching out to me, diminished but still here.

DAY 13. Beyond the white window there waited a free world of fresh air and desires and motion. It was fall. Leaves rustled among the cobblestones. Street vendors sold steaming escargot in bowls of broth, handing out tiny glasses of white wine, then shaking them clean afterward. As afternoon darkened the narrow streets, our offices would be brightly lit, my colleagues busy preparing reports for our annual fall conference.

Within the apartment, I existed in confinement usually reserved for the young or elderly, the injured or criminal. I hated the walls and the useless windows that traced the sun's arc from room to room. I longed to hide deep in the woods I had seen during my brief glimpse of the horizon, to turn invisible as a white moth on a birch tree.

As a boy, I used to explore the trails along the coffee-brown river behind our house. The riverbank smelled thick with rot and life and I pulled mussels from the mud with my eager fingers and pried them open to see the glistening whiteness that pulsed inside. I would build a fire and eat them boiled and salted, savoring their dank taste and then stacking the shells in a cairn. In July, I picked blackberries. In August, dusty wolf grapes that hung beneath star-shaped leaves.

My backpack held Cokes, beef jerky, a book, and my brother's BB gun. I wandered alone for hours, the river my only map, winding past fields of green tobacco, cattle clumped like black rocks, and farmhouses grayed by wind, rain, and years. I imagined myself a Confederate spy, noting every farmer in his fields, every salesman in his car. All were the enemy. I passed unnoticed among them.

In this childhood pastime came the model for my life, a template for the years to follow. I would wander through the world, invisible but informed, seeking out delicacies and pleasures along the way. Only now I was trapped by the enemy, held far from home, which existed only in memory.

"Americans are simply slaves to the media, always listening to what they want them to do, what to wear, what to think . . ."

I sat on the futon, only half listening to Blackbeard's latest tirade. I had studied Blackbeard closely and tried to get a better idea of what he looked like, so I could identify him when I was released. He moved quickly and gracefully, in the manner of someone in his late twenties or early thirties. He apparently had no

morals, no conscience, and no guilt for what he and his compatriots were doing. I was the guilty one, and was being punished for it.
For this and much more, I hated him. My waking hours were filled
with schemes for revenge. In my dreams, I killed him a dozen
times.

By the middle of this speech, Blackbeard had worked himself
into a state of focused anger, blaming me for the evils of the west-
ern world.

"Your efforts, Eliott Gast, have taken us all closer to the globalization that your country envisions for the world. Always luring us
to jump in the so-called 'melting pot' that would eliminate all the
differences and boundaries that protect us from domination."

I raised my hand, palm forward. "I've told you over and over, I
had absolutely nothing to do with any conspiracy. I'm an economist for IBIS, nothing else . . ."

Blackbeard waved his cigarette, then opened and closed his fingers like a mouth. "Your denials are simply annoying me more and
more. Perhaps the time has come to hurt you again." He smiled.

I said nothing.

"Anyway, we are letting the people decide what's ahead for you.
And this is being done in a truly democratic fashion, not the false
democracy that your country puts forth, this *every man is equal*
nonsense, as if the chairman of Microsoft is just the same as a man
pumping petrol in Texas."

"That's a simplification."

"One man, one vote. What could be simpler?"

I said nothing.

"We've put forth the evidence to the world and asked them to
judge you. For a price, of course." He laughed. "We are like
stockbrokers in that regard. No matter how someone votes, they
must pay us. We are gathering thousands of contributions every

day. I love the Internet. It is truly amazing." He shook his head reverently.

"They'll track you down eventually and the game will be over."

"Hardly." He shrugged. "I have a staff of computer geniuses that move our site from place to place. Black Hats, they call themselves. Young and devious. They are experts in site-jacking, as it's called. We are like vagabonds. Made so by your treachery, which tossed us from our homelands," he added, another superfluous accusation. "Today, you can be found on the Swiss government's site. I find this very amusing, given the Swiss role in international monetary corruption."

I imagined the video images of Blackbeard and me talking in the apartment alongside a map of Switzerland, pictures of the Alps, advice for tourists. "So how much money have you raised so far?"

"Why are you interested? Do you think this will somehow measure your worth?"

"No." He was right. I wanted to know that the world had noticed my ordeal and wanted to make it stop.

"The money is not the point. We are nowhere near our goal. What is truly interesting is how people are voting."

"What are the choices?"

Blackbeard shouted up at the ceiling. "Audio off!"

"Oui." The bored, disembodied voice came from one of the grates, then a click.

"They can vote to have you released. Or they can vote to proceed."

"How have they been voting?"

Blackbeard tilted his head. "So many questions. This must interest you a great deal, Eliott Gast."

It did.

"The votes so far say we should move ahead." Blackbeard held out his stack of computer printouts.

"Move ahead with what?" Certainly no one would want to see my imprisonment continue.

"The next level, of course."

"Didn't anyone vote to have me released?"

"Of course. But they are less vocal."

I closed my eyes and shuddered. Much had happened in the world to inure it to suffering. Still, I had expected that most people retained a sense of right and wrong.

"Audio on!" Blackbeard poked out his cigarette on the windowsill, then stood to issue his final proclamation of the day. "Now you know what it feels like to be in the minority, Eliott Gast. To be controlled by the cruel wishes of the majority in the same manner of the Basques, the Flemish, the Irish . . ."

His list continued. I was no longer listening. My thoughts turned to the next level and what it would bring.

♪♪♪♪♪ ♪♪♪ ♪♪♪♪♪

DAY 14. Nin, Blackbeard, and the Doctor walked slowly, silently into my room and stood in a row at the edge of the futon. I stood and scrambled toward the other room, screaming.

Blackbeard tackled me and held me down on my back, my arms trapped beneath me.

He leaned down and whispered in my ear. "Showtime, Eliott Gast. Give the people what they want." The brandy on his breath smelled of old men in cafés getting ready to go off to a day of bricklaying.

My heart pounded. The Doctor stood above me, holding two white tampons, strings dangling.

"He wants you to put these in your nose." Blackbeard failed to smile at this ridiculous request.

"What!" I pushed off with my feet, but my socks only slipped along the floor. Their arrival had caught me in my underwear.

The Doctor reached down. I twisted my head to the side, but he simply pressed my face against the floor with one hand, while pushing the tampon toward my nose with the other. A sweet, medicinal smell came from his hands. He pushed the tampon gently up my nostril, then harder, until a sharp pain came. The second one was harder to insert, and he guided it up into my other nostril with the palm of his hand, stopping only when it was deep inside. The pain I felt at first was gone, replaced by a tingling, then a numbness that spread across my entire face. I struggled to get free from Blackbeard, but he pressed harder, his grip on my arms inescapable. He bent closer and then ran his tongue up my forehead.

Blackbeard paused for a moment. "Fear tastes of white vinegar," he said. "It would taste good on fried potatoes."

The Doctor opened his black bag and rummaged around. He took out a small metal tool with a cork handle at one end and an electric cord at the other. I recognized this childhood toy, a woodburning tool. My brother and I would spend hours at the kitchen table burning galloping horses and the somber faces of the presidents into cheap pine. The Doctor plugged the cord in and we waited. I imagined that I must look like a trapped walrus.

In a moment, the Doctor pulled the cords beneath my nose, and I assumed the tampons slid out, though I could not feel them. He reached over for the woodburning tool, but the cord would not stretch to where I lay. He nodded at Blackbeard and together they slid me along the cold floor toward the wall, my undershirt rising up.

"Scream, damn you." Blackbeard whispered.

But I said nothing. I struggled as hard as I could when the tip of the woodburning tool approached, feeling its heat as it passed in front of me. The Doctor pressed firmly against my forehead to tilt my head back and steady it. I saw a thin ribbon of smoke drifting up toward the ceiling. I closed my eyes tightly. My deadened face felt nothing. The Doctor pressed close as he worked, his eyes intent, sweat dripping from his chin. Then he pressed more deeply and suddenly I felt a fire behind my face, somewhere up near my eyes. My eyes burst open and I gritted my teeth and strained with a low grunting sound of a dog.

"Make it new," Blackbeard muttered. "More action gets more money. More money means you'll be released sooner. Are you making this connection?"

Still, I stayed as silent as I could, an unwilling participant, not a collaborator. The Doctor shifted the woodburning tool and sent another puff of smoke drifting up toward the ceiling. I struggled again and Nin reached forward to help hold me still. I felt her delicate hand on my cheek. Then Blackbeard grabbed it.

"Here nurse," he said. "Your patient needs you." He took the woodburning tool and wrapped her fingers around it.

"But I . . ."

"Get to work."

I saw the fear glint in Nin's wide eyes. The Doctor wrapped his steady hand around hers and together they scoured the other nostril, burning as they went deeper, like Sherman marching through the south.

The burning within me grew. I gritted my teeth and held back the screams that burgeoned inside me. What good would they do? Nin watched her hand in horror. She tried to be careful, to hurt me as little as possible, but her hand shook as if of its own volition. Smoke rose like an odorless incense. I looked up at the faces of my torturers, hovering close as moons, while beyond, the black snakes swayed above us all, taking the latest event to the world.

DAY 15. I was sprawled on the floor where they left me after the operation, the woodburning tool still lying next to me. I reached up carefully to touch my face and felt the rough edges of a bandage taped below my eyes and above my mouth. My nostrils were filled with packing and my tongue, clotted with scabs and blisters, had dried painfully from breathing through my mouth. I rolled carefully over on my side, then rose to my feet.

The windows were bright white. It was morning, a sunny fall morning somewhere in Belgium. For a moment, I imagined that I could simply walk over to the elevator doors, which would open and take me down to the street where I would call the police.

A nightmare ends with morning. There might be a residue carried through the day, an uneasiness, or the unsettled feeling that everything was slightly off, the world out of kilter. But these effects rarely lingered past noon. My ordeal seemed only to deepen with each passing day. I remembered Nin's reassurance that I would not die. But on this morning, my face ablaze with pain, I wasn't so sure.

I barely recognized the man in the mirror, half obscured by a brown-stained dressing. I pulled at the tape carefully and lowered the bandage. My nose was swollen and bluish-red, with black marks along the nostrils like the burns of cigarettes left too long on the edge of a table. Yellow fluid dripped from the packing. I pulled at it gently and felt a pure deep pain, so strong that I quit moving and breathing for a moment to stop it. I left the packing where it was and replaced the bandage carefully below my eyes, bloodshot and wild. I reached over and carefully marked the day in the plaster with my thumbnail, each mark a day lost to pain and boredom.

I opened my mouth and saw my blackened tongue, dry and cracked. I filled my hands with water and raised them up slowly, taking a sip, then gulp after gulp, drinking as fast as I could. Bits of scabs and drainage traveled along with the water, but I drank more.

I rubbed a little water around the exposed parts of my face, then ran my fingers through my hair. I looked slightly more like myself, but damaged, changed for good. As I walked back into my room, each step jarred the pain at the center of my face so that I crept forward with my hands held out like those of a tightrope walker.

Blackbeard lay in my bed with the blanket pulled up to his chin. He ran his fingers over his face and mocked me.

"Oh, my nose . . . oh, my tongue . . . it hurts so bad, Mommy. Make it stop."

"Fuck you," I whistled, the words triggering a new blaze of pain.

Blackbeard jumped up. "You talk in your sleep, you know. Calling out for people. Talking. Last night something about a meeting in Berlin."

I said nothing.

"Perhaps you will someday spill your secrets, pass along the names of others involved in your so-called work. When you do, we will certainly be ready."

I put one hand against the wall and leaned on it. "Shut up, will you."

Blackbeard shook his head. He walked over to the windowsill, took a cigarette from the pack, and lit it. He gazed out the white window for a moment. "It's a beautiful day outside, Gast. A touch of what you Americans call Indian summer, a last few warm days before the fall rains begin. Lovers out on blankets along riverbanks. Schoolchildren out for excursions. Tourists everywhere. Unfortunately for you, you cannot enjoy this beautiful day because you are otherwise engaged." He shrugged. "A shame."

"Haven't you done enough already?"

"No. There is much to do still. Besides, yesterday's activities did not generate the level of interest that we expected." He walked closer and whispered close to my ear. "I have to ask you to work with us a little more closely. Your resistance is simply prolonging your suffering. Practice your screaming, please."

I said nothing, then asked the question that had been on my mind for days. "Why don't you just shut up and kill me now?"

Blackbeard paused, then rolled his eyes. "That would be so obvious. So crude. So . . . *Archduke Ferdinand,*" he said with great disdain. "It is easy to kill. In your country, children go to school and do it. What a typically American idea, that I should just kill you. How should I do it, Eliott Gast? Should I strangle you?" He walked over to me and put his heavy hands around my throat. Though his rough fingers only shook me slightly, they triggered new pain that made the room turn gray at the corners. "Stop it!" He lifted his hands away from my neck, then reached around his back. "Perhaps I should shoot you?" He placed the snubbed barrel of a dull silver pistol between my eyes. As its cold metal pressed into my skin, I stared straight ahead.

"Or should I set you on fire?" He put the pistol back in the waistband of his jeans and held the glowing end of his cigarette toward me.

"Or should I assfuck you to death." He sidled around behind me and began to knock against me, again triggering new bursts of pain with each jolt.

Blackbeard leaned toward me. "My thick cock would make short work of you." Then he whispered just inches from my ear. "People are certainly finding this scene intriguing and disturbing, don't you think, Eliott Gast?" He nodded up to the ceiling, as if we were actors and the audience watched from above. In the days since we first spoke, Blackbeard had taken to striding around the apartment in a much more overblown way, a conqueror surveying a captured city. He sickened me.

"No one is amused by the pain of others." I leaned against the wall, steadying myself with both hands. Closing one eye seemed to make the pain dissipate a little.

Blackbeard bent over laughing. His eyes glistened behind his mask. "On the contrary, people are always fascinated by pain and suffering, as long as it is not their own. There is a word for it. In German, of course." He paused for a moment. "*Schadenfreude*. To take pleasure in the misfortune of others. This urge is as old as mankind, a part of human nature, yes?"

"Perhaps. But people have empathy as well."

"You amaze me, Eliott Gast. A man who singlehandedly affected the lives of millions for the worse now talks of empathy. If you had any, you would not have played the role that you did in the American economic conspiracy."

I waved him away and turned toward the wall. "Go now," I said quietly, hoping that Blackbeard had an ounce of compassion.

"Oh yes. One more thing. Your nurse is off duty today."

I paused. Nin was my only possible way out of this apartment. She had hinted that she was willing to help me, but she seemed so powerless.

"She is meeting with others in our group so we can reassess her . . . personal resolve," Blackbeard said, with seriousness. "But you should not doubt her conviction. She is the most radical among us. Don't let her appearance fool you. What is happening to you was all her idea, you know."

Could this be true? A new wave of pain interrupted and I pressed the side of my face against the cool wall.

"She sends you this." I felt a sudden jab in my thigh that made me jerk forward painfully into the wall. Looking down I saw Blackbeard's hand on a syringe. He pushed the plunger quickly.

When he was done, he left the syringe hanging from my leg and walked quickly from the room.

I pulled the syringe out and threw it after him. My leg burned and I hobbled over to the futon.

I lay on my back and let whatever drug Blackbeard had injected me with take effect.

DAY 16. A lost day spent sleeping and recovering. I turned to find Nin on the windowsill at one point, an apparition. She was beautiful, the white window behind her like the clouds of heaven, the checkered scarf transformed into an ancient vestment. I stared at her in drugged pleasure, my nurse and angel, so still and powerful.

Then, when I looked back again, the angel was gone, replaced by the Doctor, who squatted close to me, his hands full of bandages splotched yellow and brown. When he saw my eyes open, he smiled and gave me a quick wave, as if we were friends off on an adventure. Of the three, I found the Doctor the most puzzling. He was both torturer and healer. I relied on his expertise, such that it was. While Blackbeard seemed to be responsible for my ordeal— and I believed that all ideas came from him, not from Nin, as he had hinted—it was the Doctor who had to carry them out. Behind his Zorro mask, his black eyes stared intently at me, charting my progress and recovery, swabbing my mouth with green disinfectant.

Even with my torturer so close at hand, I fell back asleep. I could not control the will of my body. It urged me to eat, drink, sleep— protecting me from my own mind, which wanted to do nothing at all. I sensed inside me the powerful instincts that had been hidden among the surface cravings and thoughts. My will to survive outweighed my current, damaged state. I drank water from the bottle, lay still to let time heal me, slept in the face of danger.

DAY 17. *Why is this happening?* The question that had haunted my thoughts since I first found myself in the white apartment circled back once again. I knew the reasons that Blackbeard had given. They wanted to do something new. They wanted to leave me alive but punished, as an example to the world.

But this afternoon, half dreaming from codeine, I tried to discern what led my captors on. Their anti-American, anti-EU stance was clear. What they were for was less so. During one of his rants, Blackbeard had spoken of Vlaams Blok, a group that had been in the news often during my time in Brussels. Most of my colleagues regarded them as dangerously right-wing and definitely bad for business. Blackbeard had complained that the Flemish Block was not committed enough to its cause, unwilling to do more than rattle the sword of nationalism. Perhaps Blackbeard was trying to impress someone, possibly a former colleague. I was simply part of a price war of decency and kindness, devalued and sinking lower. Although I regretted my role in this terrible game, I had to wonder what the response would be. What would it take to one-up Blackbeard? Ten online hostages? Live execution of innocents? Anything seemed horribly possible.

I slept to free myself from imagination, which I knew to be both a comforter and tormentor.

DAY 18. I found myself waiting for Nin to appear, listening for her steps. Her absence worried me. Had Blackbeard sensed that she was going to help me and punished her for it? I revisited every conversation, wondering whether something we had said had marked her as a collaborator. Blackbeard would not take kindly to dissent among his group. I imagined Nin imprisoned in another hidden room somewhere, trapped as I was, awaiting Blackbeard's lectures, his punishment.

I sat on the futon with my back against the wall, steadying myself against any movement that might trigger new pain. I had come to think of pain as an evil jockey riding my body, digging in his heels every now and then, applying the whip. Fueled by pain and frustration, I decided to stop waiting for something to happen, for some miracle to set me free. During the long, empty day I plotted and planned, moving in and out of a codeine haze that blanketed my mind but also gave me ideas, pure inspiration that would lead me out of this room. I was David to Blackbeard's Goliath. I needed a strategy that would let me bring him down fast and hard. Its elements started to appear and come together in a way that made me smile, that gave me hope and some version of courage.

While trying to spoon a few grams of rice down my throat for dinner, I heard what sounded like a jet coursing through the white sky. I looked at the painted window but could see nothing. Its distant roar reminded me that this was not the first time I had been a hostage. The first incident happened so long ago that I had almost forgotten it, relegating it to a second-tier tale for dinner parties.

Maura and I had been in Miami for a brief visit with her elderly aunt, who had an apartment in West Palm Beach and had recently fallen and broken her hip. I had work in Miami as well, a presentation at a conference. It was 1973, and I had just started with IBIS. The oil crisis had overshadowed our work. Our arcane white papers advocating reduced foreign imports, tighter monetary controls, and higher levels of business incentives seemed like so much scrimshaw—ornate but superfluous in an era of plastic. I remember driving along the ocean, the cerulean waves out of synch with the glum mood Maura and I were both in, as if a stagehand had accidentally lowered a cheery background behind a Chekov play.

On the flight home, we read, drank terrible white wine, and ate a mango we had brought along in our carry-on bag, the juice going everywhere. Far beneath us, the Atlantic shimmered, the white line of breaking waves tracing the curve of the coast as we headed north.

Suddenly, a man in the front section rose and shouted at the top of his lungs. "This plane is being hijacked to Cuba by the H.C.E.!" He waved something small and black in his hand.

The other passengers groaned and shouted, more with a sense of annoyance than fear. We had drawn the unlucky lot and were going to be the next hijacked plane. There had been so many. The man turned and spoke urgently with a stewardess, who rushed up front and disappeared into the pilot's cabin.

"Everyone else must stay seated!" His voice was too loud, his words too fast. We were not in the hands of a trained revolutionary, a compatriot of Ché or Fidel. Instead, we were being hijacked by a tall, nervous, skinny man with bushy hair, a kind of white person's afro that was popular at the time. He looked like a graduate student.

Our hijacker walked up the aisle slowly, glaring at each of us, measuring our potential to cause trouble or threaten him. There was little to fear. Most of the passengers were elderly "snowbirds" returning from a winter in Florida.

He passed quickly by the row where Maura and I sat staring down between our feet. I could smell his stale T-shirt, sweatstained at the armpits. Panic raced through me for a moment, urging me to stand up and run away, though there was no place to hide. It was easily resisted. I was, after all, at the beginning of my career, a young husband with his wife by his side. The weight of my limited responsibilities pressed on my shoulder. I would leave any resistance to someone more interested in the hero's role.

The hijacker paused in the section ahead of us, where a couple in their mid-forties sat, talking nervously. They seemed wealthy, the man balding and in a brown suit, the woman slightly over-weight and pressed into a white dress. She was hyperventilating and her ample chest rose and fell with each breath like that of a Shakespearean lover. She clutched her husband's hand tightly, but he stared straight ahead, his face white, the skin sweat-glazed, fore-head sepulchral.

"Give me that." The hijacker pointed to the wife's hand, inter-locked with her husband's. On her shaking wrist sparkled an impressive diamond bracelet.

Without a word, she took off the bracelet and handed it to the hijacker, who slipped it in his pocket.

"No!" the husband said suddenly, then looked surprised, as if the word had sprung from his mouth of its own volition.

"What do you mean, *no?*" The hijacker squinted at the husband, who said nothing, just looked away.

The hijacker raised his pistol and pressed it into the shining forehead of the husband until the flesh puckered around it. The husband stared toward the front of the plane, lines of sweat drip-ping down his face.

For what seemed like an impossibly long time, the trio stayed frozen in this posture. Then the husband made a strange gurgling noise and broke his hand free from his wife's to raise it to his chest. He bent forward and the hijacker pulled his gun away.

"Oh my God, he's having a heart attack!" the wife shouted.

The husband's eyes bulged like those of a clubbed fish and a meringue of spit trailed from his lower lip. The hijacker turned and shook his head, waving the gun across the aisles to keep us all in our seats. He leaned forward and whispered to the husband, dying now in his seat in first class. I couldn't hear what he said. Then he walked back up to the front of the plane, satisfied somehow at the death of a rich man, not exactly at his hands, but close enough. He wore a smug smile of accomplishment all the way to Havana.

We landed on a narrow, bumpy runway at José Martí Airport and stopped in front of a low hangar. A group of men in uniform approached and the airplane door opened, letting in a blast of hot air and letting out our hijacker. The soldiers spoke for a moment and he handed his pistol to them. They handcuffed the hijacker and threw him in the back of a jeep. He wore a puzzled look as he was hauled off like so much baggage. It was the time of hijacking, one every week it seemed, and he had misjudged how tired the Cubans were of earnest young men guiding 707s to their shores. I never found out what happened to him, what the H.C.E. was, or any other details of our brief ordeal, which ended hours later with our safe arrival at Dulles. The dead man sat strapped in next to his sobbing wife for the rest of the quiet trip. The red circle, where the gun barrel had pressed, slowly faded back to white while the other passengers talked loudly of their ordeal and I held Maura's hand, still sticky with mango juice.

Fear, not a bullet, had killed the passenger. In this way the mind is stronger than the body, able to end a life by simply imagining what might happen. Despite my escalating fear, I knew that I would survive this ordeal. If I were going to slump over in a heart attack or give in to hopelessness, it would have happened already. Whatever strength I had left would sustain me. All hostages live, as Nin had told me. Unless they decide not to.

♪♪♪ ♪♪♪♪♪♪ ♪♪♪ ♪♪♪♪♪

DAY 19. Taste. Smell. Gone now. Each hour of healing sealed them over beneath scar tissue. I was changed for good. I would never smell wet sidewalks after a rain, the fall leaves in the woods behind the farm, bread baking in the kitchen. And I would never be able to taste bread, wine, coffee with cream and sugar in the morning, steak au poivre, coquilles St. Jacques, ice cream in July, walnuts roasted in a skillet . . . my favorites went on and on. I had spent a lifetime collecting tastes. Even thinking of food brought about a nostalgia as painful as wounds. I sat on the windowsill and tried to clear my mind and focus on my plan for escaping this room. I needed to bring some order to the jumble of details, the sequence of events that would need to take place. But it was no use. Memories surfaced, one after the next.

When I was a skinny, quiet boy, I was uninterested in the time-honored family recipes my mother would make. Aunt Ida's pecan pie. Grandma's lemon tarts. Aunt Whatever's grits casserole. I just didn't care about tasting anything. I ate to live. Had I continued to eat the way my parents intended, I would have grown truly Orsonian by my life's midpoint, like my brother Darby. After he joined our father's firm, he ballooned to fill the space behind his desk like a deployed airbag. His hunger was of a different nature, the urge to fill unhappiness with food. Mine was more academic. I explored the realm of the senses to avoid the more difficult world of people.

When Maura and I were first married, we were too busy working to spend much time cooking or going out to meals. It was only later, at the time when most people have children, that we began to crave. This fervor came upon us with a missionary zeal. We recited magazine recipes to each other, sought out the freshest ingredients at the Eastern Market and farm stands deep in Virginia. We spent vacations walking the food halls of Barcelona and Paris. We read the food section of the *Post* with the same infinite appetite for detail as boys obsessed with baseball. I carefully measured the temperature along the fieldstone foundation of Triangle Farm and found it perfect for storing wine. I built special shelves indented to hold bottles. Then I bought cases and cases of our favorite Bordeaux, convinced that the expense would be justified in the future. Calon-Ségur. Haut-Bailly. Léoville-Las Cases. Gruaud-Larose. My lovingly recorded insights on decades of wine were brought to a quick conclusion by the Doctor's fillet knife.

I heard footsteps approaching from the other room and brightened at the thought of seeing Nin again, of sharing my plan with her, the one that would set us both free. But these footsteps were heavy and loud, without Nin's grace.

Blackbeard barged in. "Feeling better?"

His interest seemed perverse to me. He was like a cattle rancher butchering his herd piecemeal, a leg off this steer, a flank off another.

I stood and moved to the far corner of the room. "Where is she?"

"Your nurse?"

"Yes."

He shrugged. "Around. She has responsibilities beyond tending to you."

"Why are you doing this?" A small clot fell from my nose to the floor. I smeared it with my shoe, creating a carnelian accent worthy of any fine home. *Scab*, it would be called in the decorating booklet.

Blackbeard shrugged. "Because we can?"

I shook my head. "You could do anything. You could flay me alive, draw and quarter me, hang me slowly, scalp me . . . just get it over with."

Blackbeard shivered. "What a hideous idea, scalping."

"And this is better?" I pointed to my face, blackened, reddened, burnt, cut.

"You are so naive." He shook his head. "Once, there was a time when we might have hurt you and let you go. This used to be the way things were done. But now, the people want more. If you want attention, Eliott Gast, you have to go completely over the top."

"Over the top," I repeated.

"Exactly. This week an earthquake in China has killed thousands. Dissidents in Bellarus are occupying a nuclear reactor. A new virus has been identified in India, and has already infected three villages. A young mother in Liverpool killed her newborn in a microwave."

I said nothing.

"This is our competition, Eliott Gast. We must do something so audacious that people will notice it. Small acts . . . a bank robbery, a killing . . . they simply splash on the surface once and sink, like a child throwing rocks into a pond. One rock. One splash. End of

story. You, on the other hand, are continuing to set new records."
He held out his clipboard. "Millions of people have watched you
as of today. More every day. We are making money hands over
fists." He paused for a moment. "And you are too, Gast."

"What do you mean?"

"I know that you think I am a pitiless man. One who simply
enjoys watching you suffer. Like a small boy who pulls the legs
from insects." He shook his head. "But I am not truly like this. I
am simply doing my part, following my instructions."

"I would disagree with that."

"Of course you would. You are in pain. I am not. You feel that I
am responsible for your pain. Therefore you are blaming me. It is
completely logical. But perhaps your pain will be less knowing
that there is a reward at the end of it all."

I sat on the carton of water bottles. I couldn't imagine what
reward could possibly equal the amount of pain I had felt so far,
not to mention whatever lay ahead.

Blackbeard began to strut around the room, speaking in the
louder, more urgent tone that I had come to recognize as his
speaking-to-the-masses voice. He wanted to make sure our audience could hear every word. "Given your unique and important
role in our endeavor, I have decided that you should have ten per-
cent of all our gross earnings." He leaned toward me, hands open
and outstretched. "It is very generous, isn't it?"

"It's sick. Only a very twisted mind would find it generous."

Blackbeard walked closer. "Audio off!" he shouted. "You are
already wealthy. And if you play your cards right during the
remainder of our time together, you could end up with millions.
My advice? Practice your screaming, Gast. You have to scream very
loudly to be heard over the incredible din of the world. You have
to go over . . . the . . . top."

"Go away." I waved my hand in front of me.

He turned at the doorway. "You are a fool. Your time in the trenches of the American economic conspiracy has left you remarkably out of touch. You have no idea what the world is really like, no imagination."

Blackbeard shook his head for a moment, then rushed off like a businessman on his way to an urgent meeting.

He was wrong. My imagination was filled with plans. I wanted to grab his infuriating mask and rip it away. I would turn the tables and reveal him to the world. The same cameras that recorded my every move would capture his image, if only for a moment, and broadcast it to the world. Certainly someone in our audience would recognize him, identify him. Then he would have no place to hide. The world would be his prison. I savored this plan for revenge, so slow arriving.

DAY 20. The apartment was invaded by a dozen people, a work crew of some kind that clustered around a short ladder near one of the ducts. They all wore jeans, dark shoes, white T-shirts, and green alien masks with huge eyes and stunned mouths open in ovals. One of the aliens at the top of the ladder held a sheath of cables and the others poked at it with screwdrivers. When I walked to the doorway, they turned, acknowledging my presence briefly. In the center of their eye holes, I could see narrow, squinting glances. They were surely the Black Hats, the young computer geniuses that Blackbeard was so proud of. They turned back to their work.

I drifted over to the windowsill, then toward the bathroom. I was unimportant, a human clown in their technological circus.

The burns, my swollen face, had no effect on them. It was just my mask, no more real to them than their own.

They were intent on their work, whatever it might be. Perhaps the images of my ongoing torture were not of high enough quality. Or maybe now I would be broadcast in stereo. I took a chance and assumed that the cameras were off while they were working. In the bathroom, I reached up and grasped the showerhead with one hand and tried to turn it. It wouldn't budge. I reached up with both hands and turned it a few inches. The strain sent pain shooting across my face and blood trickled from one nostril. In a few moments, I had the showerhead off. It was about the size of a baseball and made of heavy steel coated with shiny chrome. I tucked it under my shirt and pressed my arm down to hold it in place. I stepped out of the shower and pulled the curtain closed. I slipped the showerhead beneath the mound of damp towels under the sink.

One of the Black Hats pushed open the door abruptly with his foot and looked in. I turned to the mirror and pointed at my bleeding nose.

"I need to wash up," I said, then reached for the faucet. He left.

I washed my face slowly. For all I knew, the cameras were back on again.

When I came out a few minutes later, the Black Hats were through with their project. The one at the top of the ladder replaced the cables far inside the duct, screwed the grillwork back in place, and climbed down. Another dutifully folded the ladder and carried it under his arm. Their work complete, they left like a team of alien plumbers.

At the door to my room, the last to leave paused for a moment and gave a backward glance. Perhaps in that moment, he imagined what it was like to be trapped in this room, awaiting what the next level might bring. Or maybe he was just checking to make sure they brought all their tools with them.

The room was empty again. I tried to smoke a cigarette, my first in days, but the smoke dried my tongue painfully and I couldn't taste it. There had been enough burning. I stabbed out the cigarette, an action broadcast to viewers perched in front of computer terminals around the world.

What possible interest, much less pleasure, could they be taking from my imprisonment? Being held hostage was numbing and terrifying at the same time, as if I sat beneath a dangling piano, waiting for it to fall. Meanwhile, the piano played the same song over and over again—a boring song of sleep, food eaten from cartons, long hours at the whitened windows mulling over my plan. Blackbeard issued his diatribes. The playing would become intense in brief bursts with the arrival of the Doctor. Otherwise, the days were spent waiting beneath the piano, watching its shadow sway around me.

DAY 21. "Goedemorgen, Eliott."

One of the black snakes dropped lower to capture Nin's quiet voice. I said nothing, not wanting to seem glad to see her.

I gazed out at the whiteness where anything could be imagined. She moved over next to the windowsill, her long print skirt rustling.

"You are angry at me?"

"Where have you been the last few days?"

"They had other work for me," she whispered. "My time is not my own."

"He says this is all your idea." I watched her eyes between the scarf's folds.

"Hardly," she whispered. One of the snakes dropped lower. She stood up straight. "Of course it's my idea. You must be punished for your role in the American economic conspiracy. In this way, we can send a powerful message to the world." She said these phrases in her own careful dialectic tone—acquired, perhaps, during her recent re-education. I knew she didn't mean what she said. She was simply trying to make sure she didn't get in any further trouble.

"You told me you would help me," I whispered. "I think I know how you can. We need to talk."

"I am not in a position to do that right now," she whispered back.

A black snake lowered from the ceiling.

"Our purpose is clear, our resolve unshakable," she said curtly. "We are telling the world that the American economic conspiracy will not be tolerated any longer."

I rolled my eyes.

"Argue with me, Monsieur Gast, s'il vous plait," she hissed through her teeth.

I thought for a moment. "What is happening here will in no way affect national policy. This is a personal assault."

"In a way, yes, but your work makes you a public figure. You represent that vast apparatus that your government has put in place to control the world economy."

"I represent only myself," I yelled. "And your attempts to turn me into a kind of symbol are truly misguided. Why not kidnap a senator?"

Nin shrugged. "No one cares what happens to a senator."

"Your indifference truly astounds me. Imagine if I were your brother. Or your husband. How would you like to see him mis-treated like this."

There was a long pause and Nin's eyes stared, mine stared back. "I have no husband," she said quietly.

So much shouting made my head throb, and I had to sit down on the floor.

She broke off and walked toward the door. "Our files on you are open to the public now," she said. "They can decide whether you deserve this treatment or not, Monsieur Gast."

She marched from the room and I stared after her. I picked up a half-full food carton and threw it, making a convincing splash of cold broth along the wall. Nin was my only hope for escaping the apartment, and now she seemed to be under as much scrutiny as I was. How would I tell her about my plan? Who could possibly sur-vive under such a close watch? Who doesn't carry something with him that he wouldn't want revealed to the world—a scheme, a secret, a sin?

When I was eight, my brother and I turned into businessmen. We melted down lead weights and molded them into soldiers, which we painted and placed in cedar boxes we decorated—a forest for a medieval knight, the Tower of London for an English guard, a line of bushes for a Confederate sharpshooter. We took our soldiers door to door through Roanoke and sold them for fifty cents each. Darby and I did a good trade with the boys in our neighborhood and started to make money, which wasn't very hard since my father had given us the molding kit for Christmas and the local body shop let us take as many lead weights as we could carry away.

Our proud father marched us into the Old Dominion Savings and Loan, where a special account was set up for our "business." We were both issued passbooks stamped with the same blurry purple ink I sometimes saw on the white fat of supermarket steaks. After that, my father let us wander farther and farther from home in the afternoon, and our expanding sales route gave us license to go to previously forbidden parts of town.

One afternoon we found ourselves in Simms, where the houses tilted and the lawns were threadbare as attic rugs. We knocked on the front door of a corner house that looked slightly better kept than the others. A big-shouldered black dog with dripping jowls was tethered to the porch swing, but it only came forward to sniff us.

The door opened slowly and a thin black boy about our own age stood behind it. He wore a dirty short-sleeved shirt and tan shorts. His feet were bare and I could see that his toenails were as long as claws. A gray cat rubbed around his narrow shins.

"Whatch you want?" His voice was surprisingly deep. Black wraparound sunglasses hid his eyes and he kept his head cocked to one side when he spoke.

My brother and I glanced at each other, both realizing that he was blind. Our pity quickly gave way to a more immediate question—what would a blind boy want with a lead soldier? For a moment, we felt foolish and embarrassed. We both thought of running away. But then Darby spoke. "We're selling lead soldiers. They're fifty cents."

The boy stuck his hand forward. His fingers were pocked with pink scars, his fingernails long and untended. Darby put a soldier in his hand, a Union rifleman, I noticed. Perhaps he felt this would be more compelling. I was already backing away from the porch. We should have gone over to the new developments on the outskirts of town, where the houses were close together and filled with scrubbed white families with salesmen fathers, mothers who were Brownie leaders. The pink pads of the boy's fingers rubbed over and over the soldier as if he were trying to decipher it. Finally, he stopped rubbing and bent down to set it carefully on the floor.

"I'll take one." He turned and walked back into the house, trailing his hand along the wall. I followed him with my eyes and saw the long grease mark that bisected the house about four feet off the floor. When he retraced that line a few moments later, he carried with him a women's cigarette purse with a pack of Kools and a Zippo lighter poking out of the brown suede. He turned over the case and reached into the other pocket, fishing out a folded wad of bills. His fingers peeled apart the ones, and tens, then carefully handed us a bill from the stack.

"Here." He pushed a twenty at me.

I looked at Darby. He shrugged. I turned back and stared at the boy's hands. My honesty was being tested by God and a blind black boy with greasy fingers who couldn't tell one bill from another. I looked again at my brother, who kept his face perfectly still, abstaining from this particular test of character in a way that I immediately found cowardly. Perhaps it was greed, perhaps it was anger that my brother didn't at least offer his advice—a quick shake of his head would have steered me toward honesty—but I took the twenty. Then I handed the blind boy two shining quarters bearing the grim, neutral face of Washington, who could never tell a lie.

"Thanks," I said. And I meant it. Thanks for the money. I could already see the purple stamps in the passbook edging up. Thanks for letting me get away with something for once. My brother had always been the troublemaker, but now I had disgraced him and claimed his role as the baddest. We turned and walked back down the shattered walkway, then ran all the way home.

That evening, Darby told our father every detail of the event, adding a white lie about how he had warned me not to take the money. The next morning, I found myself back at the house in Simms. I handed the blind boy the twenty and a set of a dozen of our best soldiers. Then, while my father watched intently from the convertible, I mouthed a laughably self-abasing paragraph he had helped me write. In a choked voice, I admitted I had stolen the money deliberately, that I had sinned, and that I hoped that God and His goodness would rescue me from my low tendencies. I had taken advantage of an affliction and for that had demeaned not only myself, but my family, the state of Virginia, and my race.

At the end of my speech, the blind boy picked up the soldiers, pocketed the twenty, and gave a small smile. For a moment I wondered if the joke was on me. Darby said he was almost positive blind people could tell the difference between bills.

The screen door slammed closed and the blind boy's fingernails scraped back along the wall into the dark center of the house. I got in the car, relieved and drained. My father said nothing as we drove away, then stopped the convertible so fast my head bumped the dashboard.

"Go tell 'em what you did." He pointed at the next house, a gray-boarded farmhouse with rusted metal chairs jammed on the porch.

I rubbed my forehead. "What? They don't know anything about it."

"They will now." He reached over and opened my door, then pushed me out with his boot.

In all, I played the role of penitent more than a dozen times, enduring the laughter and empty stares of strangers. Once my father's lesson was complete, it burned into my soul so thoroughly that it could never be erased. It was my first true sin.

It was no wonder that people held in captivity eventually confess to anything. Here I had hours, days even, to do nothing but revisit my mistakes and wonder if they were to blame for my present state. It was hard not to cast Blackbeard as St. Peter, judging all real or imagined strayings from the way of the righteous. In my youth, there were girls I lied to in order to bed them, or car them, or field them. At Princeton, I turned in my thesis, as well as a list of a dozen SDS members from Campus Club. For this, my thesis advisor thanked me and added that my government thanked me, too. At the language institute, I cheated on a Spanish test to qualify for an embassy position. That cheating led to a year-long internship in the Santiago embassy, where I taught the young, spoiled sons of Pinochet's henchmen how to speak English and blow smoke rings and do the famed Tiger railroad cheer. Then there was IBIS, and the work that Blackbeard and the others found so reprehensible. But my sins didn't end there . . .

Nin rushed into the room quickly. "We don't have much time, Monsieur Gast," she said.

I sat up and buttoned my shirt. "Time for what?"

"To talk in confidence."

I pointed up at the ceiling. "In confidence?"

"I have a friend who is handling the documentation this afternoon. He has promised that the system will experience a brief loss of transmission." She glanced at her pink watch. "Starting now."

"Please help me," I said. "Get me the hell out of here. Please, do whatever you can."

She shook her head. "All I can do is tell you what I know so you can prepare."

"Prepare for what?"

"For what comes next."

"Don't they have their money yet?" I had hoped that money would draw my time as a hostage to a close.

"They have reached their goal and more," she said curtly. "This is where our group is in disagreement. Some of us, and you cannot mention this to anyone . . ."

I nodded.

"Some of us think that this has gone too far already, that the threat of what we were doing was more effective than the actual doing of it."

I said nothing, but the possibility of an end to my ordeal lifted my heart. I took dissent within Blackbeard's ranks as a good sign.

"We are convinced that continuing beyond this point will be self-defeating. We have sent our message. Any more of this would be unnecessarily cruel and repetitious. But others are insistent that we proceed and make more money, reach more people."

"And keep me here longer?"

"Yes. And I must say again that none of this was my idea, Monsieur Gast. Our group is diverse by its nature. Various factions are at odds with others."

"Just help get me out of here."

"There are too many controls, too many safeguards." She glanced at her watch. "We are wasting valuable time discussing the impossible."

I opened my mouth and pushed out my blackened tongue at her. A pulpy crack the color of a ripe persimmon ran down the center like a faultline of pain. Every word I spoke or breath I took brushed a nerve.

She gathered her scarf around her. "My God! Stop it."

"This is your work. If you aren't proud of it, then apologize for it."

The apartment was quiet for a moment. I could hear the air whirring out through the ducts, where the black snakes were still for once. The glass windows ticked softly like a radiator, as they did late in the day when the sun began to fail.

Nin turned to me, her brown eyes glistening with tears. "Of course I'm sorry. I never wanted to hurt you. I'm so very sorry."

"Then help me."

She nodded. "I'll do what I can."

I knelt next to her. "I want to unmask your pirate friend."

"He's well known to the authorities. This has made him extremely vigilent about secrecy. You'll have to kill him first."

"I can stun him for a moment, but I'll need your help. Together, we should be able to bring him down and show his face to the cameras."

"The cameras are not always on," she said. "Besides, there are often many people around him."

"Then I need you to tell me when the time is right."

"I'll give you a signal . . . I'll raise my right hand high."

"Good," I said. "We'll need to do it when he least expects it. I'll hit him on the head."

"With what?"

"Something. A weapon. I'm working on it. He'll be surprised, stunned. That's when we can pull down the mask."

"It will be very dangerous."

"I won't let anything happen to you," I said, unsure how I would keep that promise.

"What do you want me to do?"

"Open the doors. Show me the way out of here."

Nin stared at me for a moment, then leaned forward and pressed her fingers against my forehead gently. She held them there for a moment, then drew back again, as if surprised by her own actions. Her touch sent tears to my eyes.

"We have only a few more moments, Eliott," she said softly. "I must tell you something else."

"Yes?"

"You must know that what comes next will be very difficult."

"What could be worse than what they've done already?"

"Believe me, it is worse." Nin turned to me and I saw her dark eyes darting behind the folds of her scarf. "Let me end with the most important point. I cannot stop the others from continuing. But I can tell you this. Your body makes you a monkey. Your mind makes you who you are. Your mind will survive intact even when your body is damaged."

I smiled thinly. "I'd prefer to have both. Body and mind. They tend to work well together."

"Of course. But our situation now is less than ideal." Nin paced around the room. "They are committed to moving ahead to the next level."

"Because there is so much money coming in?"

"This is one of the reasons. But there are others . . . more personal."

Before I could push for more information, one of the black snakes lowered slowly from the duct. "Audio on," said a bored voice.

" . . . and as I suggested," Nin began in her schoolteacher tone. "You might use the time you have to reflect on your life."

"I have done little but that," I shot back, playing the role of angry hostage. It was true. There were no distractions anymore. I couldn't read without being reminded of the absurdity of reading. I couldn't exercise without realizing its futility. The hours slipped by in a lost sort of way, as if I were on a long airplane flight with an uncertain destination. Our conversation gave me new hope. With Nin's promise to help me, I was no longer alone.

She handed me a packet of codeine tablets. "These are to be taken one every four hours. No more."

"Or what . . . I might accidentally die peacefully and deny the world the pleasure of watching me suffer?"

"I have said enough for now. You have your instructions." Nin stood, her eyes distracted. She had taken a risk talking to me, and seemed unsure whether she had gotten away with it. She walked toward the other room, trailing one hand across the back of my neck as she passed. It had been weeks since I felt the hand of another, except for when I was being tortured. Her touch, even so fleeting, brought tears to my eyes again, and I turned my face toward the wall to hide them.

DAY 22. Old bottles. Drowned dogs. Water-logged *Playboys*. Darby and I used to walk the creekbeds and riverbanks looking for whatever might have washed up. We found a wad of money stuffed in a pair of pantyhose once, fifty dollars or so, and that kept us going for weeks. I suppose this was the ongoing theme of our childhood, looking for money.

On a warm October afternoon, I was far ahead of Darby and too busy looking at my feet to notice that we weren't alone anymore. Three older boys I'd never seen before trailed me on the riverbank. They all wore denim jackets, black jeans, and boots. I could hear a jangling of wallet chains. Every now and then, one would shout something in a thick, backwoods accent or throw a rock at me. I pretended not to notice. Then they rushed ahead and stood in a line ahead of me. I tried to walk between them, but they tripped me and bent my arm behind me.

The boys dragged me quickly across the creekbed and pushed

my face down in a scum-covered pool edged with green. I held my breath and waited for them to let me free. Then, as I ran out of air, I opened my eyes and stared through the tobacco-colored water blotted with darker leaves. Bubbles ran from my nose like silver droplets of mercury set free from a thermometer. My chest ached and when I arched my back toward the surface, the boy who held my hair tightly intertwined in his fingers pushed down even harder. I could hear muffled laughter through the water. I struggled as hard as I could, and then I couldn't anymore. I breathed, and the tainted water made me choke and convulse so hard that the boy let me loose.

Or so I thought. One of the boys stumbled across the creekbed, his hand over a bloody patch on the back of his head. Darby had finally caught up. I lay on the creekbed and watched my brother chase the boys with half a brick in his hand. He threw it and hit the last boy in the small of his back, propelling him into the woods. They moved on, a pack of wild dogs.

Darby walked over to where I lay. "Leave you alone for a minute and you go and get yourself in a bind." He wiped my face with his shirtsleeve.

I coughed and spat out the sourness in my mouth.

"They're from Gallensberg, mark my words. They'd drown you for smokes."

"I don't have any smokes."

"Then for the fun of it. The way farmboys do with kittens."

I didn't like being the comparison. "I never did anything to them."

Darby shook his head. "Doesn't matter. Being innocent never meant you wouldn't get beat up." His brow furrowed for a moment. "Matter of fact, it generally means you *will* get beat up, as far as I can tell."

"Next time I see them, I'll kick their ass."

Darby shook his head. "Next time you see them will be in the newspaper when they get arrested for doing something stupid. Until then, steer clear of them."

We walked back up the creekbed, me spitting, my brother checking the banks for any other boys from Gallensburg. We never walked there again.

In the empty room, I could hear my breathing and nothing else. I stalked through the apartment, checking for anyone else who may have come in. My brother wasn't here to protect me anymore. I was on my own.

I stared at myself in the bathroom mirror. As a boy, I had spent hours studying my face, entranced by the fast flow of emotions, one after another like the shimmering reflection of leaves on a bedroom wall. Young boys are the world's most avid narcissists. As the years passed, I avoided mirrors, displeased with what time was doing to me. I had a new reason to look—to survey the damage.

Exhaustion and spartan meals had turned my face thinner and etched lines along my forehead and at the corners of my eyes. If I held one hand over my mouth and nose, I could almost pretend I was the same as before, just jet-lagged or hungover. But when I looked in my eyes, I saw a deadness that no amount of exhaustion could create. I saw the eyes of a dog that has been hit too many times by its master. They were lifeless and roving, looking for danger, as if this was all that the world contained. Then I moved my hand away and the change was clear. I counted a half dozen pink and black burns along the edges of my nostrils.

Opening my mouth wide sent the pain flooding back and I clenched my hands tightly into fists to keep from screaming. I gave a codeine tablet a practiced flick beyond the blackened crust and drank from my hands. There were no clean towels, so I dried my hands in my hair. The apartment, so carefully tended during my early imprisonment, had fallen into disarray. The floor of the bathroom was layered with dirty towels, bloody shirts, and half-empty food cartons. The sink was crusted with scabs and pus. Once vigilant, my captors had turned sloppy. No one even noticed the showerhead was gone, packed in a sock and hidden beneath the towels. I left everything where it lay. What was the point of keeping my cell tidy? With Nin's help, I would be leaving soon. When the time was right.

DAY 23. I lay on my back and examined my hands in the dull light. The simple gold wedding band was encircled by skin, wrinkled and almost as lined as my father's was when Darby and I lowered him in the ground a decade ago. My fingers were long and bent slightly at the ends as if ready to type a report.

Once my hands were part of my attraction, along with my manners, careful observations, and tendency to listen rather than talk. On our first date, Maura and I had drinks at the Advocat, a dark, quiet bar in Princeton where undergraduates rarely went. The bar smelled of wood polish and decades of cigarettes. On the tin ceiling, small fans circled in the warm air. Glasses of beer glowed along the bar and the narrow room seemed to be a portal north to New York or east across the ocean to Europe, where other ancient bars waited.

With undergraduate sophistication, we drank gin and talked about the war in Indochina, our impending graduation, watching each other's faces for reflections of ourselves. Around us, old men in suits read the *Packet* and talked to the bartender, blind to the nascent romance at the corner table. She laughed at the things I said. Just sitting near her made me smile. Or as Yeats put it, she *gave the moment wings.* A professor we knew came into the bar and the spring wind blew down Witherspoon Street and through the open door to lift Maura's napkin from the bar. It blew toward me like a leaf. Without looking, I raised my right hand and caught the napkin deftly between two fingers. Maura pretended not to notice, but years later would remind me of how graceful I was then. In just a few years, I had transformed myself from a boy who walked the creekbeds of Roanoke into a polished, urbane Ivy Leaguer. I reflected on the cruel math; I was older now than the men in suits who sat in the bar that freighted spring afternoon when my hands moved with grace.

Above, the black snakes emerged to capture me as I was now, face pale and bloodless, nose marked by burns, tongue pink and scabbed. Is this what the world wanted to see?

I was tired of waiting, of doing nothing. I stood on the food carton and reached up into one of the ducts and pulled out one of the snakes. I turned the end toward my face and the red light flicked on.

"This whole . . . the entire . . . there's no reason for this to continue."

Unlike Blackbeard, my monologue was unrehearsed. "Imagine what this feels like."

I stuck out my tongue.

"Or this."

I moved the camera closer to the burns around my nose.

"You can see me. You've seen what goes on here in this . . . this hellhole. I know that. But that isn't enough. Just watching me. It's like you're looking out an apartment window into another building where something terrible is going on. But you're not doing anything about it. You're not making it stop. So you're a collaborator. You're giving them an audience. If you quit watching, it will all stop. If you keep watching, it will keep going. It's really that . . ."

The red light flicked off.

I threw the end of the camera into the wall. Over and over I smashed the black bulb into the wall until bits of glass filled my palm. I opened my hand and watched the blood course from tiny cuts that didn't hurt at all.

DAY 24. Places I would rather be. Sitting in the kitchen of our farm, drinking coffee and talking to Maura at the breakfast table. Walking through Brussels on the way to a meeting. Driving out in the country on a warm spring day, the thawing earth giving off the smell of worms. Anywhere far from this white-walled cell.

People could see the details recorded by the black snakes—the disarray of the rooms, the opaque windows, the occasional visits from Nin. But they couldn't know what it was really like here. At times, the apartment seemed deep within the ground, a bunker beneath the world where the normal rules did not apply. Other times it seemed trapped in the clouds, the white glow of the windows giving off a celestial light.

Sometimes I was sure that this was all a dream, that if I blinked my eyes enough it would vanish. But other times, no amount of hope or pretending could make it disappear.

DAY 25. I heard the sound of an airplane overhead again, on its way to Paris, Madrid, Frankfort. It ground on for almost a minute. I thought of the last times I had been on a plane, and wondered how long it would be until I was on another. In isolation, the ordinary turned luxurious and strange. To fly on an airplane seemed impossibly complex, requiring a sequence of events—purchasing a ticket, packing a suitcase, getting to the airport, going through customs—that I would find difficult to complete in the correct order. How had I kept it all straight? Why didn't the incredible freedom I once had stall me with its infinite choices? Just a few weeks ago, countless Sabena flights from Brussels to Washington were a regular part of my life.

Going home last month, the plane had landed early. A tailwind across the Atlantic shook drinks from trays the entire flight. I took a cab from Dulles and spent this stolen hour in the Potomac, a narrow basement bar on 19th and H, crowded and beer-soaked. Harsh voices made requests one after the next—a beer, a pack of cigarettes, change for the pay phone. I was too exhausted to go look for a more peaceful place to wait. Maura was meeting me for dinner at the St. Regis in an hour. Later, we would drive back to the farm for a long weekend of rest.

I drank a glass of terrible red wine and watched the two televisions at either end of the bar. One showed a woman I recognized standing on the steps of the Capitol with a microphone jammed in her face. She was a lawyer who used to work at Commerce and had turned lobbyist. The sound was off and I couldn't hear what she had to say, not that I much cared.

I turned to the other television and saw two tanned young boys slumped on the seat of a red motorcycle. There had been a horrible accident. A voiceover told how they had swerved off a road in Thailand and become impaled on a thin guardrail that pierced both through the chest. They were still alive, arms flailing and heads wobbling as emergency workers in yellow uniforms examined them ineffectually. The show cut away to the two boys seated on a talk-show couch. They looked serious as they told the host of their ordeal. Then came more footage of the emergency workers cutting the railing with blowtorches that glowed green. Freed finally, the two were carried to a waiting ambulance, still impaled,

Siamese twins conjoined by steel. They were shirtless, and blood flowed freely as water from their wounds, their hands clutching the railing as if they could pull it free.

I shuddered. For a moment, a shadow of pain burned in my own chest. Around the bar, people talked and smoked, looked up occasionally to watch the boys in the operating room, where the steel rail was removed slowly as a splinter. Then they were on the talk show couch again, raising their shirts to show off the white scars that radiated across their chests. In the bar, people reached for their beers, ate peanuts sticky with sugar.

I sensed evil hovering in the bar along with cigarette smoke. We all saw the boys writhing in pain. Perhaps some thought it was horrible. But we didn't feel the pain ourselves. What a different world it would be if we felt everything we saw. Not all men felt empathy. Something inside protected them and let them watch suffering.

I was just as ambivalent. In less than an hour, I would be sitting at a table in the St. Regis dining room, trying to decide between the 1985 or the 1986 Pichon-Lalande, the sautéed dayfish or the halibut with artichoke hearts. The pain of the two impaled boys would be nowhere in my mind. The sufferings of one life—real or imagined, small or large—were enough to wrestle with.

So it was with my own ordeal. No doubt people were watching me as I paced the cement floor, the cameras bringing my bruised and disfigured face into their suburban homes. When the iron was pressed into my tongue, the woodburner pushed up my nostrils, they may have looked away. They may have felt a twinge. After it passed, they could still taste and smell. No damage was done to them. They ate and slept as if nothing had happened. They moved on.

I was still here, waiting for the next event. Nin's forewarning did no good. There is only a moment between when the doctor tells you a shot will hurt and when the needle enters your arm. Imagine that moment stretched out for days, with nothing to distract you from thoughts of how much it will hurt, how thick the needle will be, how inept the doctor is. Any possible distraction was swallowed up by the fear of what lay ahead.

DAY 26. A dull clanging came from the other side of the apartment and suddenly Blackbeard stood at the doorway. In one hand he held a cowbell, in the other a thick paintbrush. He marched in, hitting the brush on the bell, which I noticed was actually a cheese grater. A group of aliens followed him, green rats to his Pied Piper. One carried a bag of ice. Another carried a white plastic cooler. The last one held the silver bowl in front of him, hitting it with another paintbrush. A cold wave passed through me. The sight of the bowl—the same one Nin had held beneath my chin—sent me running to the corner of the room. I pressed back against the wall, jabbing a chair in front of me.

"Stay the hell away from me!"

They came closer. The Doctor entered the room last, still tying his white coat around his waist with a thin belt. Nin came in the room last, lingering back near the door. Her hands were at her side. She gave a small shake of her head.

"Greetings, earthling." Blackbeard laughed and the aliens huddled around him. I stayed in my corner.

"Fetch." He pointed toward me and the aliens sprang forward, hands out.

I glanced at Nin again and she shook her head firmly this time, eyes narrowing. This was not the right time to set our plan in motion. Still, I couldn't just stand by and wait for whatever pain they had in mind for me. I hit the first alien with the chair and he fell back on the cement. As I swung again, three more surrounded me and pulled the chair away.

"Get away from me!" I sent one to the ground with a kick between the legs. Nin was right; there were too many of them to fight. They surrounded Blackbeard like bodyguards. They pulled me forward and forced me to sit on the floor.

As I caught my breath, I heard the ice pinging in the metal bowl, one cube at a time. When it was full, one of the aliens grabbed my wrists and thrust my hands deep into the ice. It felt good for a moment, the metal on my palms, the white cubes around my skin. Clean and cool. My hands turned painfully cold and I tried to pull them out.

Blackbeard leaned closer. "If I were you, I'd leave them in."

I tried to pull my hands out. The aliens pressed them down. Away from our struggle, the Doctor took a small glass jar of what appeared to be apricot jam out of the white cooler. He opened it and smelled it, pulled his face back quickly. He put the lid back on and looked at me for a moment, his gaze steady. What did I look like to him? A figure to be pitied or to be punished? Nin had said that the group was divided, and I could only hope that he was on the side less inclined to continue.

Blackbeard nodded and the Doctor pulled my hands from the ice. He dried them carefully with a plush towel bearing the emblem of the Georges V, a hotel in Paris where I had stayed several times, I recalled pointlessly.

The Doctor leaned down next to Blackbeard and picked up the cheese grater, made of steel with a white plastic handle at the top. Standard issue for any kitchen. He examined the four sides. The first had only three slots on it to peel off slabs of cheese, I supposed. He shook his head and turned the grater. The second side had dozens of slots, each curving upward like an open mouth.

When Maura and I made lasagna, we used this side of the grater to shred mozzarella. This side he rejected as well. The third side was punctured by hundreds of tiny sharp holes. This was the side we used to turn a slab of aged Gouda into a bowl of shavings thin enough to melt on warm pasta.

This side seemed to please the Doctor. His mouth crinkled a little and he gave the grater a little toss, catching it deftly. Then, with complete nonchalance, he reached out, pressed my wrist against the floor, and began to scrape the grater over the back of my right hand.

Shocked, for a moment I didn't struggle. I watched as tiny pink pieces of skin fell to the floor. The pain started breaking through my numbed hand.

"Stop it! Stop it now!" I tried to pull away, but they held me firmly. The Doctor drew the grater down my hand in careful strokes, efficient as a carpenter. With each stroke, he pulled off tiny bits of flesh and sent blood coursing from my knuckles, five deep red circles among the pink wounds.

"Stop it! Please stop it!" I screamed.

"Good," muttered Blackbeard. "Finally, a little action around here." He patted his shirt pocket and wandered off toward the windowsill to look for my cigarettes.

The Doctor stopped for a moment and I kept screaming. Then he turned my hand over on the blanket and scraped the grater down my palm, doubling the pain. I tried to pull my hand back, but they held it even tighter. I screamed as loud as I could and pressed my eyes closed, as if not watching what was happening to me could somehow stop it. But the Doctor continued his efficient carpentry, grating the palm and pads of each finger until they were thoroughly raw. I opened my eyes for a second and saw what appeared to be a hand formed of raw hamburger.

One of the aliens passed the Doctor the pot of jam. He held out his hand and another assistant placed the paintbrush handle in it. The brush was black and short bristled, the kind we used to make signs back at the farm. Yard sale. Squash and tomatoes for sale. An arrow to direct dinner party guests to the back patio. The Doctor began to paint my palm carefully, his brow lined with concentration. Whatever he put on my hand felt cool and soothing at first, then began to burn. I screamed as the chemical burn grew stronger, making my arm shake involuntarily.

Blackbeard leaned toward me, cigarette stuck in the mouth hole of his mask. "Bio-polymer," he whispered. "It's made with sheep's plasma and resin. Usually they apply it underneath skin grafts to achieve the right kind of bond. Incredible stuff." He turned to me. "And expensive, too. Unless, of course, you steal it from a hospital."

"Just stop it now. Stop it! This is too much!" My shouting echoed through the apartment.

Blackbeard nodded, then pointed to a spot on my index finger that the Doctor had missed. "Yes, perhaps. But what is too much anymore? We have an obligation to our audience." Blackbeard glanced up at the ceiling, where the black snakes dangled far from their ducts.

"What about me?"

Blackbeard exhaled and rolled his eyes. I was being old-fashioned again.

"A little emoting would be good right now," he said. He reached over to my left hand, still intact, and jammed it deep into the ice. Then he seemed to remember something and yanked out my hand. He pulled my wedding ring from my finger. It came off easily—my fingers were thinner. He held the ring out to me, then thought better of it and pushed the ring into the mouthhole of his mask. I saw the pink of his thick tongue, unmarked by any scabs. He swallowed.

"You just can't beat the taste of American gold," he shouted to the black snakes. "Nothing like it." He leaned back his head and laughed, then turned to me and whispered. "If I find it in my shit, I'll be sure to tell you."

The Doctor took my left hand and pressed it down on the towel, spotted now with blood, bits of flesh, and the orange substance, thick as the glue that Darby and I used to put together model airplanes when we were boys. My whole body shuddered and I was going to be sick.

"If you're going to vomit, be sure to turn to the left." Blackbeard said. "That's the best camera angle."

As the Doctor began to scrape the top of my other hand, I saw the apartment turn gray at the corners. The aliens hovered, evil spirits in green. Sweat coursed down the Doctor's tight face as he worked. Blackbeard's eyes stared from behind his mask. Nin paced in the background, hands over her face. Bits of color swam before my eyes like fetid water beneath a microscope. I opened my mouth to say something but crumpled instead toward the corner.

"Don't pass out on us now, Gast!" Blackbeard shouted. "The fun's just started."

But it was too late. The apartment turned darker and then vanished, taking everyone with it.

DAY 27. After my junior year in college, I took a summer job at a resort on the Virginia coast. I did the requisite things college boys do in summer—brought waitresses to my lonely hotel room, sat out on the beach late at night, drank lots of beer to counter the oppressive weight of the future. As part of my job, I bussed dishes from the tables of the businessmen attending "conferences" that seemed to involve eating, drinking, and golfing.

On my first night in the kitchen, I dumped a full tray next to the dishwasher and headed back through the swinging door into the restaurant. I saw something in the vat of steaming rinsewater that made me stop. At the bottom of the vat lay a shining silver dollar. From my days collecting coins with Darby, I knew it was a Standing Liberty, a particularly beautiful coin. I squinted into the vat but couldn't make out the date. I looked around me at the rest of the kitchen staff, all sullen year-rounders, all at least a decade older. They seemed too preoccupied with their work to notice as I pulled on the thick rubber gloves next to the sink and pushed my right hand slowly into the water.

The water was close to boiling and dosed with bleach to kill off bacteria. My fingers moved toward the coin, just a silvery shimmer at the bottom now. I could feel the hot pressure of the scalding water around the glove. Then as I pushed one last time, the water washed over the top and down to my fingertips. I jerked my hand out, but the water held the glove to my hand so tightly that I couldn't get it off. Instead, I hopped around the kitchen doing what was known as the rinsewater polka, the kitchen staff told me later. One by one, the cooks turned and applauded me, the latest in a long line of summer help to fall for the silver dollar, soldered to the bottom of the tank decades ago. Finally, one of the waitresses helped me peel the glove off of my hand.

The next day, my fingers were red and blistered, my forearm pink up to a line just below my elbow. I wore this burn for the rest of the summer, charted its transformation from red to pink to peeling skin to scar.

Now both my hands burned with an intensity far beyond a simple scalding. It was as if the thick gloves from the resort kitchen had turned molten and adhered to my skin. The jelly had congealed to a solid, rubbery finish. I could move my hands, but slowly and painfully. They were thickened, cured of grace. I would never catch a bar napkin in midair again.

The spots and scars and familiar creases in my skin's terrain were gone like topsoil washed away by a flood. My hands were yellowish gold in color, flecked by bright bloody patches and whitish places where the grater had taken off the skin all the way down to cartilage. Sitting in the center of the living room, I looked at my hands dispassionately, since they didn't seem to be mine, perhaps part of a Halloween costume. Encased now, my fingers had turned clumsy. I could move each one, but couldn't pick up my cigarettes or raise a bottle of mineral water. When I ran my finger along the floor, I could feel nothing. I raised my fingers in a cathedral, all touching at the fingertips. The familiar warmth was buried, gone.

Sitting among the dirty clothes and rancid food cartons, I started sobbing. I cried not for my lost feeling, which I couldn't even begin to contemplate yet, but for my lost wedding ring. It had been on my finger since the June day in 1973 when Maura and I were married.

It was a wild, disorganized wedding, kept intentionally simple, since neither Maura nor I liked formal occasions. We stood on the public beach in Carmel, our group of relatives and graduate student friends huddled around us as the sun set over the Pacific. Darby had been officially deputized by the State of California to perform the ceremony, and wore a small-town justice of the peace getup of his own creation—a white shirt and black bolo tie, jeans, boots, and a silver badge. I can still picture the ring shimmering in the last of the day's sun as he handed it to Maura and she slid it on my finger.

We were broke, so our rings were simple gold bands inscribed with our initials along the inside. Any jeweler could replace my ring for less than I used to spend on lunch with clients. That something innocent and simple had wound up so thoroughly defiled seemed awful. A fate I shared. It was my recognition of my complete helplessness that set me crying.

After a few minutes, the tears ran their course and my anger at Blackbeard rose up again. I remembered his greedy mouth, swallowing. Nin was right—he was consumed by his own vision. I couldn't imagine that it was shared by the others in his group. Yet the Doctor had complied in his methodical way, grating at my knuckles like a Parmesan rind. The others, too, had not stopped for a moment in the entire procedure. Perhaps they believed I actually deserved this mistreatment.

No cause was righteous enough to condone what they were doing. If I were being held hostage by psychopaths who had escaped a Belgian prison, their actions would have at least had an explanation. But such cruelty from seemingly intelligent people, well versed in politics, economics, and technology, seemed impossible.

I stood in the shower beneath water as hot as I could bear, trying to scrub the biopolymer from my hands. It was no use. It stayed tight on my skin, fused there forever. This was to be my first day without feeling, gone from my hands now, but not from my mind.

DAY 28. "Excellent, excellent, excellent." Blackbeard held out a thick set of print-outs. "All I can say is keep doing what you're doing."

I said nothing and merely continued cleaning as well as I could without a broom, or hands capable of holding one. I was sick of how disgusting the apartment had become. I kicked the trash around, tidying up like a good hostage, amazed that I was still here, unsure that I would be leaving anytime soon, or at all. How would I unmask Blackbeard without using my hands? The corners were soon thick with debris of my imprisonment—food cartons, balled-up clothes, the silver wad of duct tape that originally bound my ankles, a bandage from my mouth, the blood darkened now to chestnut.

I stopped cleaning and stared at Blackbeard, trying to find any hint of humanity in his glinting eyes. He looked away.

"The audio is off for a few minutes," he said. "We can speak frankly."

Again, I said nothing. I had realized that any discussion with Blackbeard was wasted. I remained a simple pawn to him. Only by denying him any conversation could I attempt to diminish him.

"You are being broadcast to the world from the United Nations site for the next couple of days," he said. "Until they figure out how to kick us off." He leafed through the pages the way my father used to page through the newspaper, looking for interesting items to read to me at breakfast. "Our audience particularly liked yesterday's performance. Contributions are up. We are well on our way to our goal."

I knew that greed and public attention kept Blackbeard going more than any cause. But I said nothing. Protest would simply fuel Blackbeard's bluster, his self-righteousness.

He rustled through the papers. "Here's an interesting aspect, Eliott Gast." He found the page he was looking for. "There's been a turn of the tide in your favor. Many people are asking for your release. There have been highly visible campaigns in the press. A *Washington Post* editorial. Statements by the Belgian government. And your wife has been very active in gathering support . . ."

I looked up suddenly and met his black eyes, shining behind his stupid mask. This news was the first I had heard of Maura in weeks. I had imagined her at the farm, tracking my condition on her computer, making calls to try to get me released. I should have known that she would go beyond that. Maura never shied away from a challenge. It was her hard work that had turned our farm from a ruin into a home. She was doing what she did best, organizing. Except now the cause was her husband.

"Don't you want to know more about what's happening?"

Of course I did. But I said nothing.

"I'll give you a little more." He moved closer. "Despite the efforts of your wife and others, more people are making donations to see our project continue than to stop it. Any teenage boy who can get his hands on a credit card number has been contributing money . . . and intriguing ideas about what we should do next."

I said nothing at this news, which might or might not be true. It seemed too horrifying to think that anyone would want to see my ordeal continue.

Everything had its price and someone willing to pay it.

Blackbeard shrugged. "Now for the good news. We've found that there is a high percentage of return visitors. People are seeking you out, following you like fans. You are truly famous now, Eliott. We have become a recognizable brand."

He smiled at me, as if this alone was worth the scorching of my tongue and nose, the grating of my hands. How I wanted to reach out and grab the thin plastic mask with my deadened hands and pull it away. I wanted to kill him, to return to him all he had done to me, to put my thickened fingers around his throat and choke him until he turned limp.

Blackbeard stood. "I'll leave you to your thoughts."

He leaned down as he passed me. "If I were you, I'd keep talking. I'd talk as much as I could," he whispered. "Because soon, it will be very, very quiet for you, Eliott Gast. That I promise you."

DAY 29. The Doctor held my hands in front of him, examining them for infection. The red patches at my knuckles had darkened. The grated areas had turned the speckled red and yellow of maple leaves in October.

"When you look at what you've done, how can you not think about how this must feel?" I asked quietly.

The Doctor looked around the room, then whispered. "Because they are not my hands."

It was the first time I had heard the Doctor speak. His voice was soft but resonant, and he spoke completely naturally with me, as if we were old friends from university. We had, after all, been through a lot together.

"But what if they were?"

"Then I'd be glad that someone like me was making sure all was healing well. Everyone else here would ignore you and you would become infected. They're too busy with their computers, their Internet. They know nothing else. I call them *e-tards*."

"So you provide the illness, then the cure. That's the kind of doctor you are?"

He gestured for me to open my mouth. "I am not a doctor." He took a bottle from his bag and swabbed my tongue with green disinfectant. "My training is in electrical engineering."

"I'm just another machine to you. One you can break and then fix."

He closed the bag. "Not exactly."

"Why are you doing this?"

He walked away.

"*Why* are you doing this?" I shouted. The disinfectant tasted like nothing, just burned my mouth. I swallowed and the burning traveled down my throat.

I heard no answer, just the steps of the Doctor crossing the apartment and entering another room, where the others huddled around their computers, charting contributions and monitoring me, so incidental to their plan.

In the afternoon I gingerly grasped one of the snakes, wrapped it about my arm, and pulled it from its duct. I placed it on one chair while I sat in another. The red light glowed as the snake took in audio and video. It was the tunnel that led to the world, one that

106

could carry the message that had been composing itself in the back of my mind.

"You have seen me for several weeks now." My voice was scratchy at first, my words trailed by the whistling of my damaged tongue.

"Sometimes I have been walking around. Other times I have been writhing in pain. At all times I have been a prisoner. I realize that there are efforts under way to gain my release, and I am thankful for them. I want to thank my wife for doing what she can to help end this pointless and barbaric charade. I want to thank the Belgian government for their efforts. But I need to clear up one matter."

I paused for a moment. My tongue ached. Other snakes trailed from the ducts and glowed like party lights.

"Although I have denied any wrongdoing so far, I want to tell you the so-called secrets that have landed me here. Then you can more accurately judge whether they merit this treatment." I pointed at my face, then held up my hands.

I paused for a moment, wondering what to say next. "For more than a decade before the establishment of the European Union, I was active in delivering inducements—large sums of money—to key individuals within certain governments. You may remember that some countries were reluctant to join the union. My close involvement with foreign business groups and economic officers made me an ideal point of contact for an activity that our government could not perform through normal diplomatic channels."

I paused for a moment and imagined the reaction of my coworkers at IBIS. What a shocker to find out that their Gast—faithful practitioner of the dismal science, liaison to the middle managers of the world—once had another role. I saw Alec Moore on the phone, distancing the organization from my work.

"The specifics are unimportant at this point, but I can assure you that the sums were enormous," I continued. "They provided the funding necessary to shut down opposition groups and to pay off bureaucrats with nationalist leanings. There was plenty left over to contribute to the personal fortunes of our recipients. In this way, we paved the road to unification . . . and to a global economy, I suppose."

I shifted in my chair. "I am sure that these funds were also used to harass and jail anti-unification activists. These activities were certainly wrong, and I assume they are the reason why I am here. But they are not out of keeping with events at other junctures in history. Change dictates its own price, as they say, and we were willing to pay it. And why not? What better way to win a game than to buy it?"

My half-smile faded when I realized that my amusing aside might be misinterpreted as imperialist bravado. "I firmly believe that a united Europe benefits Europe as much as it does us. Everyone comes out better for it. It ensures parity among all the European markets, which, as you may recall, were all but paralyzed by outmoded regulatory systems."

People were already forgetting the old Europe, with its tedious border crossings, expensive consumer goods, currency shortages, and Balkanized business environment that kept trade to prewar levels. The old ways of doing business in Europe were ridiculous and fraught with corruption. Any sub-cabinet trade minister in Rome was able to jack up Italian tariffs on American goods simply because his brother made leather handbags. So we fought fire with fire. We were corrupt and deceitful. But I didn't go into more detail. I already sounded too much like an academic crank, going on about markets and regulations.

"Our work also guaranteed American access to a profitable, unified foreign market," I continued. "By putting American interests first, I'm certain that I brought about undesirable personal and political results that were not clearly for the betterment of Europe." Actually, I was sure that what we brought about would have happened anyway. Money is the yeast of the world, but I didn't bring this up to our audience either. "For that, I sincerely apologize."

I sat quietly for a moment and waited for my strength to come back. I hadn't spoken so much in so long that speaking tired me. In truth, my words were neither sincere nor an apology. I hadn't renounced anything I had done or any of the policies that led me to do it. I never would have brought it up if I hadn't found myself trapped in an apartment awaiting imminent pain. Even my former contacts would understand. Not that anyone cared. Our hidden operation was dismantled shortly after unification. My contacts had moved on to Singapore, Hong Kong, and Beijing while I retired to continue my work at IBIS. Mine was a dead story, unlikely to cause a stir in any sector—political or the press. What we had done was done, and nothing could now undo it, this *marriage of cousins*, as Blackbeard so aptly put it. There were new courtships to arrange.

I stared at the red light on the tip of the black snake. Images of my tired, damaged face coursed down the wire, up through the ductwork, into the computers and out to the world, which I hoped was receiving my revelation with a certain amount of compassion.

"More," said the dulled voice from the ceiling.

"What?"

"Say something else."

My chair creaked as I leaned forward. "Punishing me for my work is like beating the paperboy for bringing bad news," I said. "I did not authorize the bribes. I delivered money to corrupt officials, but certainly didn't tell them what to do with it. I am not responsible for all that I am being blamed for."

"More, *s'il vous plaît.*"

I paused for a moment. "Okay then. I single-handedly dreamed up globalization. I like the World Trade Organization. I hate French cheese because it smells. I eat at McDonald's three times a day, sometimes more. I am intent on burning down the rain forest and building luxury condos there. On weekends, I club sea turtles and dolphins and seals . . ."

The red light on the snake clicked off. I smiled, then kicked over the chair. I had gotten my message across.

A trio of aliens entered the room quickly. Two shoved me toward the bathroom while the third stood on a chair and replaced the camera deep in the ductwork. No doubt they were rebroadcasting my greatest hits—the Doctor scorching my tongue, me sprawled on the bathroom floor vomiting. I smiled, certain that I had gotten a new message across to the world. What was going on in this room was as ridiculous as it was cruel.

"How did you like that performance?" I asked.

"We put on music when you got boring," the alien said as he shoved me into the bathroom. The door slammed shut and the lock clicked.

I saw my sweat-glazed face in the bathroom mirror and smiled. I had won a small battle, but the ordeal was continued. I brought my glazed hands up to my face and rubbed my eyes with unfeeling fingers, rough as a gardener's grasp.

DAY 30. "Your speech has proven to be very popular," Nin said.

"Is that so?" I sat on the floor and ate from a carton of cold white rice, each grain hard to chew and flavorless.

"The newspapers are making a great deal of it."

"There must not be much going on." At first I had craved a newspaper, a television, something to keep me connected.

Nin shrugged. "Intrigue is always popular."

"There was little intriguing about it," I said.

"So you didn't wear a trenchcoat and carry around suitcases full of American dollars?"

I laughed. "Usually, I carried a suitcase with a change of clothes and a couple of books to read while I waited." I recalled days spent in hotels when time turned nearly as tedious and slow as it had in my apartment prison.

"And the money?"

"It was in my head."

"Money in your head?"

"Yes. A ten-digit Swiss bank account and a one-word authorization." All the high technology in the financial world came down to two men speaking words and numbers, millions of dollars encoded in our conversation.

"Weren't you tempted to keep a bit of it?"

"No. I'm not particularly acquisitive, unlike others who have to have more and . . ."

She raised her palm. "They are angry enough already," she hissed. "Do not push your luck."

I laughed. "My luck? My luck has been invariably bad so far." Of the thousands of people involved in the push for globalization, only I, a footsoldier, was being punished for it.

"You have to be more grateful." Behind her scarf, Nin's eyes gave no trace of this being a joke.

"Grateful? For what?" I threw down the rice container, the larval grains scattering on the ground. "For the delicious food. For the constant pain. For being turned into a monster." I held up my shining hands. "For the enchanting company of someone who is as powerless as I am to make it all stop."

She held up her hand again. "Yes. For all of this and more. You need to change your ways of thinking, Eliott Gast. It's time to focus not on what you've lost, but what you still have."

"Oh, it's easy for you to be so glib. You're not the one being tortured." I stalked around the apartment looking for my cigarettes.

Nin pointed to the red pack on the edge of the futon. "This much is true. But you are missing my point."

I shook a Dunhill from the pack and lit it, then pulled the dry smoke along the side of my mouth, avoiding my tongue. "And your point is?"

"I have already told you."

"Right, that bit about my mind. How I should be glad to still have one. Well, after a month in this room, with only you and the others to talk to, I'm not sure I do." I dropped my cigarette and tried to pick it up, but succeeded only in moving it around the dirty floor. I brought my foot down on the cigarette and ground it savagely into bits of tobacco and paper.

I turned back to Nin. "What do you want, anyway? Did they send you to find out more about my brilliant career? There's nothing else to tell. I have nothing else to confess."

Nin stood. "I asked to come here."

"Why?"

"I enjoy your company, Monsieur Gast," she said. "Your thoughts interest me."

"Likewise," I said. "But there's only one problem. I'm losing my mind. Do you hear me? I've had enough!"

"I told you that I'd try to help you," she whispered, moving closer.

I held up my ruined hands. "You call this helping?"

"I'm sorry," she said quietly. "There was nothing I could do." The black snakes lowered and she turned away.

"Just get me out of here," I shouted at her back. Nin paused when she reached the doorway.

"Have faith, Eliott," she said. "You will leave soon. But there is still much ahead of you."

"Then let's just get it over with." I waved my arms wildly, making my fingers come alive with pain, all that they could feel at this point. "Bring on the torture. I'm already broken. Cut out more parts. Scald me more. Take it over the top. It's easy! It's easy!"

Nin left and I ran through the apartment, throwing chairs, clothes, whatever else I could pick up. Like a monkey in the zoo. Winded and sweaty, I fell to my knees, then pressed my forehead into the floor like a child or a believer bowing to Mecca. Only I had no beliefs and I couldn't be sure what direction I was facing. All I knew was that I had to get out.

♩♪♩♪♪♪♩♪♩♪♪♪♩♪♪♪♩♪♪♩♪♪♩♪♪♪♩♪

DAY 31. I stood a few feet away from the metal doors, tightly closed, which led to Blackbeard's world. In my dreams, I imagined these doors opening. I would walk through them, then descend in the same elevator that had brought me here so long ago. It would be Indian summer outside still and I would feel the warmth on my face. I would pause in front of the building and breathe for a moment, the air scentless but warm. Then I would walk calmly to the edge of a cement plaza, where Maura, my brother, Alec Moore, and an assortment of friends and business associates waited. I would shake hands and miraculously the amber gloves would fall from my hands and the nightmare would be over. The public's gaze would be drawn elsewhere and I would retreat to our farm, to recover, read, and forget.

I kicked the door over and over. In repetition I found a certain comfort—the slow cocking back of my right foot, the swift push forward so that the toe of my shoe met the metal door head-on, repeated over and over like a mantra.

The rhythm summoned up my weekly jog around the Reflecting Pool, when I used to dodge tourists, roots, and the shit of geese that huddled on the grass. I gave in to memory as I kicked, and returned to the flat, elegant strip of land, so pure and incorruptible. As I ran the long, worn path toward the Washington Monument then back to the Lincoln Memorial, I often sensed the older city beneath the traffic and gray office compounds. In this dank, oceanic place of rutted roads along the Potomac dwelled the souls of revolutionaries and men of ideals. My runs were a kind of penance, reminding me that my work with IBIS meant nothing. When I died, my history would go unrecorded on any plaque. While I lived, I could only run wheezing among the monuments of far greater men. There were few better ways to stay humble.

It was difficult to stay moody while running. The rasp of my breathing filled my ears. My heart pounded. Sweat limned the neck of my sweatshirt. One summer afternoon the steps of the Lincoln Memorial were crowded with visitors, each climbing the long, steep marble steps then turning reverent as they walked inside, as if the spirit of Lincoln resided here. There was a rally going on at the base of the monument, where white and black teenagers sat in neat rows in the sun, a catalog of indifference. A small, energetic man in a blue suit paced nervously in front of them. He spoke down into a microphone he cradled. "You have to take control of your life. That's what the Gospel tells us."

A distant "Amen, Praise Jesus!" came from the audience.

"And that means taking control of your financial situation. That's what I'm here to tell you about today. The journey from spiritual riches to new financial security."

Martin Luther King had delivered his famous speech here. But the man in the blue suit didn't have a dream. He spoke of the common desire of our time—personal wealth. I stopped for a moment to listen, glad to walk after two laps.

"It is said in the Gospel that you cannot serve God and Mammon."

"Amen." There were a few older people in the assembled crowd, teachers perhaps. Their responses kept the man in the blue suit going.

"I am not asking you to serve God and Mammon."

"That's right."

"I am asking you to serve God by achieving your personal best, by letting the light perpetual shine on you and deliver God's graces to you."

"Amen."

"And to accept God's graces, you have to be ready. You have to have a plan. You have to have a system for personal financial security."

I turned and started running again, afraid that I might start laughing out loud if I heard more. I was not a believer, but I was fairly certain that achieving financial security wasn't a major theme of the scriptures. I ran away from the crowd, down the long path lined with maples and benches.

I had dealt with money for so long and on such an abstract level that it had become meaningless. After delivering millions to my contacts in Europe, the small transactions that fill every day—buying a cup of coffee with a dollar, handing a cab driver a ten-dollar bill—seemed ancient and quaint to me. We were all caught up in larger tides than we could fathom. Savings, financial planning, the American obsession with the stock market—these were all like attempts to stop a flood with a carefully built wall of matchsticks.

We could only be truly secure by taming the larger swells. At least, that was how I justified my work.

At a point in his midlife, every man has to reconcile his own unimportance. For some, this leads to a realization of wasted years and subsequent depression. For others, it leads to an attempt to inject false meaning into what they have done.

I was in the second group. I told myself that my work at IBIS had connected hundreds of American firms with trading partners in Europe, generating billions of dollars in trade. Then there were my clandestine chores. There was nothing very heroic about waiting in foreign hotel rooms, venturing out for dinner or a newspaper. During each trip, I spent a total of less than ten minutes with my contacts, just enough time to pass along the information I had. After completing my task, I would walk down the city streets. No one passing me knew that I had just committed an act that might change their world. Businessmen made millions. But I had done something of deeper importance, *in the nation's service.* In these patriotic moments, pride flourished, then quickly faded. I had only delivered numbers and words. I was less than a footnote.

I started my last lap. As I circled the end of the plaza, I could see the rally breaking up. About halfway down, I saw another man running down the steps. Only serious runners sprinted on the steep stairs. He was younger than I, gaunt as a marathon runner, his legs spindled with muscles. He was shirtless and wearing green running shorts. A school group crowded the steps of the monument, and the jogger had to dodge through them. Halfway down, he lost his footing. Perhaps he was trying to avoid one of the students or misjudged a step. He fell forward, flying above the steps, face jutted forward, eyes closed.

"No!" I shouted. The runner fell for what seemed like minutes, parallel to the marble steps, arms outstretched. He hit the steps with the sound of a melon being dropped, then rolled down the stairs head over heels, tainting the marble with his blood. His crumpled body came to rest face down a few feet from the rally.

"Is there a doctor here?" The man in the blue suit rushed over. "Oh Lord God have mercy!"

The crowd rushed forward to see the runner, arms moving in slow motion. I shook my head at the unfairness. One moment confident and healthy, the next moment . . . The man in the blue suit knelt down to pray. I turned and kept running, leaving the crowd behind me to gawk and shudder, to feel thankful that this didn't happen to them.

Certainly that was what our audience wanted from me as well— another bloody performance. But today wasn't to be their day. Instead, they had to watch me kick a metal door again and again. My pointless kicking went on so long that my foot ached and the pain on my tongue rekindled. I pressed my tongue tightly in my mouth, then spat on the wall, making drips of red and yellow.

After about an hour, I sat down on the floor in front of the door for a moment and breathed deeply, feeling the pain in my face fade a little. Beyond the white windows, the light was failing. It was fall, a time of early darkness, the warm lights of bars so inviting, the cobblestones damp beneath the streetlights. A cigarette, coffee, and brandy used to mark the end of my day. A Hoogaarten beer and a bowl of mussels with leeks would be my dinner. Then back to my apartment to read and drink wine. That time seemed to belong to another century.

I raised my hand to scratch beneath my nose, where the burns had come alive from my sweat, the skin pocked and yellow like a quince left on a branch. The cold surface of my hard fingertips still strange to me, and I imagined that I could peel off the amber gloves I wore now and be free. But the Doctor had done his work well, and these hideous gloves were mine forever. Fueled by a new dose of rage, I stood and started kicking again, sending the dull rhythm echoing across to where I envisioned Blackbeard and the aliens surrounded by cables, monitors, computers, and their own debris, probably not so different from mine.

In a few moments, I heard footsteps behind me.

"Stop it," Blackbeard said.

"Why?"

"You're boring our audience."

"Good. Fuck them."

Blackbeard moved over to my side. I could see he held the silver pistol in his right hand.

"Turn toward me."

I kept kicking the door over and over.

"Now!" He pressed the short gun barrel into my temple.

I turned slowly and pressed forward until the cool tip of the gun rested directly between my eyes. I pushed hard against it.

We stood so close that I could see Blackbeard's dark eyes, bright with anger, could sense his malevolent charge. I was no longer playing the role of good hostage. Perhaps he was tired of our whole charade too, and ready to end it all with one quick pull. Then again, I *was* the golden goose.

"You're too much of a coward," I said loudly. "You hide behind your mask, behind your ridiculous speeches. Everyone watching knows you're an idiot." I raised my eyes to the ceiling, where the black snakes dropped slowly.

"Good," whispered Blackbeard. "Now we're getting somewhere. Say something worse."

Instead, I said nothing. I remembered the dead man on the plane from Miami, how the pistol in his face had scared him to death. But at that moment, I felt none. After all that had happened, fear was not part of me. I had already been so violated, nothing new could scare me. I reached out suddenly and grabbed the bottom of Blackbeard's mask but the plastic slipped from my clumsy fingers.

Blackbeard backed away quickly. "Damn you," he hissed, then pushed me up against the metal doors. When he strode across the apartment, I turned and starting kicking again, sending a defiant rhythm throughout the fading apartment.

DAY 32. I sat on the toilet wondering whether the world was watching me shit. Certainly someone was. The black snakes kept me constantly available to whoever wanted to turn on their computer and find me. It was late and I was half asleep, wanting to finish so I could get back to the futon. I felt something strange and looked beneath me. Delicate white cloth—a bandage, a piece of cheesecloth—stretched into the bowl. When I reached down and pulled it, I felt a strange tugging inside, a quiver at the end of my spine. The white threads were woven carefully into a fine gauze that I couldn't break. In the harsh light of the bathroom, I saw that it stayed white and pure, glowing like a mantle even in the disgusting toilet, which hadn't been cleaned since my arrival. I had shit, vomited, and bled into it. Now the white rope dangled unsullied into the water. I pulled again and felt the strange tremor inside.

"What have you done to me now?" I shouted up at the ceiling.

"What have you done to yourself?" came the response.

"I don't know what you mean."

There was no answer.

"What is this?" I pointed to the whiteness.

"Your soul. You have sloughed off your soul."

I woke on my futon, face glazed with sweat. No white rope stretched from inside me. My soul, such as it was, remained inside.

DAY 33. Blackbeard, Nin, and the Doctor appeared at the door in the morning, followed by a group of aliens.

"Ta-da," Blackbeard did an elaborate bow and swept his arms before him. Two aliens trudged forward.

"Allow me to introduce two of my associates. They will be assisting us in today's event, which is of a somewhat delicate nature."

I ran toward the bathroom and slammed the door. Inside, I held the knob tightly and pulled as hard as I could with my hands. I looked up at the ceiling and one of the black snakes emerged slowly, red light glowing.

"Stop this. Stop this!" I shouted. "Tell them to let me go. You have to do it, now . . ."

Someone pulled the door and the knob almost slipped from my grasp.

"I just want to go home. Maura, if you can hear this, call Alec Moore and tell him to pay them what they want. Get the money from IBIS. Just tell him to make this stop . . ."

I reached down beneath the pile of mildewed towels and found the sock I had hidden there, the heavy showerhead in its toe. I hid my weapon under one arm.

The door yanked open and the aliens grabbed me. They dragged me over to the corner, where the Doctor, Nin, and Blackbeard waited.

The Doctor smiled and gave a small wave, as if we were friends who hadn't seen each other in awhile. Nin stood silently beside him. Between the folds of the scarf, her eyes stared ahead without any trace of emotion. She gave no sign that this was the right time to strike. I couldn't wait any longer.

I tore away and swung the sock overhead as hard as I could. I hit an alien in the side of the head, sending his mask flying as he fell to the floor, then scrambled out of the room. I swung again and hit another on the shoulder, keeping him at bay. I turned toward Blackbeard, my arm cocked back to swing the heavy sock. He held up his hands and hunched over to protect himself. In one quick tug, Nin could reach over and pull off his mask. I paused, waiting for her to pull the mask off. She stood motionless beside him.

I swung the weight as hard as I could, the heavy end arcing toward Blackbeard. From the floor, one of the aliens reached up to dig his fingernails deep into my other hand, breaking the skin's crust and sending me to the floor in a spasm of pain. The sock whirled across the room, then ricocheted off the wall like a way-ward comet.

I lay on the floor and screamed. Aliens grabbed my arms. One came forward to kick me in the head, making the room come alive with sparkles of pain. Over my screaming, my ears rang with a high, pure note.

"Finally, some excitement." Blackbeard held up the sock and took out the showerhead. "And a spark of creativity, too. I'm impressed. And I'm sure our audience is too. Everyone wants you to be a hero, Eliott Gast. They're cheering for you." He threw the showerhead across the room. "Unfortunately, you won't be hear-ing them."

He tossed a pillow from the futon onto the floor with an elab-orate gesture. "For your comfort," he said. He nodded to the aliens and they forced my shoulders down, centering my head on the pil-low. Blackbeard sat on my knees, facing me.

"Despite the recent excitement, this part will require concentra-tion and a calm mind, Eliott Gast. Otherwise the pain will be unbearable and the procedure . . . unsuccessful."

My chest heaved and I couldn't catch my breath. I tried to twist free from the aliens. More seemed to have appeared, their young, undamaged hands holding me down.

"I've confessed already. I've given you everything you wanted. Now leave me alone!"

I turned to the side and saw the Doctor open his bag. He searched and took out two small blocks of wood, one painted red, the other blue. They were from a set of building blocks, the kind children built into towers or castles. Each had a small hole drilled in its center that left the wood splintered and fresh. I pictured the Doctor taking them from his son's playroom before coming here today, carefully selecting the right size, promising to return them.

The Doctor reached into his white coat and took out two identical icepicks with dark wooden handles. What good were icepicks anymore? What purpose did they serve except to wound? My heart started to race.

The Doctor pushed the tip of an icepick into the red block, then one into the blue block. With a small tape measure, he checked how far each point stretched out, then adjusted the red block, inching it carefully down. He nodded, handing one of the assemblies to Blackbeard and one to Nin.

Blackbeard leaned forward. "Any last words?"

"It will be a pleasure not to hear your ridiculous voice ever again," I said tersely.

Blackbeard shook his head. "Very brave, Eliott. Defiant to the last. Our audience will enjoy this. Anything else?"

I said nothing.

He looked at Nin. She leaned forward and whispered quietly, her lips close enough to brush against my ear. "I'm so sorry, Eliott. I couldn't . . ."

Blackbeard pulled her roughly away from me. "Enough love

123

talk. Here are my last words." He leaned to my other ear and the sharp edge of the mask scraped my chin. "Never forget that you have brought this upon yourself," he whispered. "You are not innocent, Eliott, you *fuck*."

Blackbeard held the blue block close to my right ear, while Nin knelt to my left, positioning the red one. I could feel the tips of the icepicks in my ear canal like mosquitoes on a summer afternoon. Then I saw the masked face of the Doctor above me. He looked directly in my eyes, holding my gaze with a seriousness that made me stop struggling for a moment. In that moment, he placed his hands on both of the blocks and pressed them together as if clapping his hands. I heard a loud pop and then another—the sound of a balloon bursting. A red flash of pain seared through me.

I saw the Doctor's lips moving but couldn't hear anything. He moved away. Blackbeard rose as well, laughing. Nin lingered for a moment, looking at me, her lips still. She gave a brief shudder.

Then the anger rose up in me. They had deafened me, taken away my ability to hear the swirl of voices, the world. I was already completely powerless and they had diminished me further. I was only a specimen to them, squirming in a filthy petri dish.

I kicked out at the aliens, catching one in the stomach and pushing him across the floor. I shoved another away, then picked up the red block and rushed at Blackbeard, his broad back retreating across the room, day's work done. The moment played out in slow motion. Someone may have shouted a warning but I heard nothing. My feet slapped on the floor in silence.

Blackbeard turned slightly as I ran closer. I jammed the icepick into his shoulder, the block stopping it from going in farther. He opened his mouth but no scream came out.

Blackbeard turned and swung at me with his other arm, his fist connecting with my jaw. Blood gushed from my nose and the pain in my mouth blazed again. As I raised my hands to my face Blackbeard tried to swing again but the Doctor was behind him, pinning him. He pulled the icepick from Blackbeard's arm and held his hand over the red circle spreading on his white shirt. They stumbled out of the room together, Blackbeard's mouth moving, the Doctor urging him on. Nin stood behind them at the doorway, her eyes squinting.

In the bathroom mirror, a small trickle of blood dripped from each ear. The pain was dull, but when I opened my mouth, it was unbearable. I screamed for a moment but heard nothing. I looked in the mirror. *My God, I'll never hear anything again.*

I mouthed the words but couldn't hear them. I quit talking to stop the pain, but kept thinking of all that I would never hear again. The wind. Chekov plays. Glasses clinking. The crowd along Boulevard Anspach. Ravel's *Miroirs*. Maura's voice . . .

I panicked and rushed through the apartment, tripping over boxes and slamming into walls. I wanted to outdistance this pain and loss, the way a child runs away when he scrapes his knee. At the metal doors, I pulled back my foot and kicked, but heard nothing. I pounded on the doors with my deadened fists. I screamed. How tragic I must have appeared to the world in these moments, raving like Lear as I turned and smashed through the apartment in utter silence, destroying everything I could put my hands on. I broke everything in the apartment into the smallest pieces I could make. All in silence.

DAY 34. Silence took me underwater and built a second prison around my first. It changed me more than any of the Doctor's other work. I pushed the futon into the corner of my room and sat pressed up against the wall to keep anyone from surprising me. I was afraid that if I slept they would come back to finish, damaging me even more, if such a thing were possible. I knew that it was.

I looked around the room with the fast glances of a cornered animal. Only by keeping my eyes open would I know when they came to blind me. But after hours of watching, I saw only the black snakes swaying slowly above me, lulling me to a half-sleep filled with thoughts of water, soothing water running from the tops of skyscrapers, warm water turning the streets of Roanoke into rivers. The brief reverie took me back to the flood year, another time of silence and pain.

All spring the skies had stayed gray and rain came with every afternoon. Riverbanks flooded, bridges were washed away, and we were out of school for a month because the buses were axle-deep in river mud. When the rain finally stopped in late May, it was too late to finish school, so we were all set free. Others had lost their houses or farms. Darby and I gained our freedom. Needless to say, we thought only of ourselves.

Despite our father's warning never to go to the quarry, every day we went there. He told us of high school kids who drank too much beer then jumped into the water and smashed their skulls on rocks hidden just beneath the surface. He told us that there were rusted hooks and cables under the water left over from the quarry work. *Widowmakers,* he called them.

We swam to the bottom to see the kings. We had found them one spring day, waiting for us in the cool depths. They drew us back to the quarry all through the floods and the hot summer that followed. Darby and I were not afraid as we eased into the water from a slanting rock. We spat in our masks, puffed to clear our snorkels, took a deep breath, and then we were on our way down. The pale skin of Darby's nascent belly looked green underwater and I used to call him Lochy. I was the Squid, because underwater

I swam on my side using a flailing stroke that I was convinced moved me along faster. I must have been ten years old. Dad was at work all the time, our mother had moved back to Richmond, and we were off doing things we weren't supposed to do—what finer way for boys to spend a summer?

Older boys kept cases of beer tethered in the depths of the quarry to keep it cold. At first, this was the treasure we sought. We dove down through the bubbles trailing behind us. The bottom was jumbled with granite blocks dumped in when the quarry shut down. Each block was covered in a greenish moss that softened the edges and felt alive beneath our hands. The tumbled stones formed triangular hollows where they fell. In the first, we found a rusted beer can and a fishing lure. Darby pointed up to the shimmering surface. He always ran out of air before me, but we had promised to stay close. In a few kicks we were at the surface, sputtering and breathing the warm air. Across the water we saw boys swimming. Darby squinted. "No women, Squid. Just a bunch of our kind, dammit."

"Maybe we should try a little closer to the shore," I said.

My brother shook his head. "They're down here. I memorized where they were from last time."

"You sure this is where we were?"

"Positive."

"But all the stones look alike."

"Trust me, I know they're here. Take a deep breath."

We took a deep breath and plunged back down.

At the bottom, we swam past the slabs, then peered down between them. Darby nodded quickly and gave me a thumbs up. I moved in closer, careful not to let my flippers stir up the silt.

Suspended in the water, we stared in fascination. Between the rocks lay a figure no bigger than a baby, curled on the brown moss.

Time, fire, or some other powerful force had changed him into a new being formed from leaf skeletons, tiny bits of plants, and dirt. His eyes were closed, mouth in a neutral line, face drawn and sallow. On his head was a pointed hat of twigs. Darby pointed at me. I nodded. It was my turn.

I reached out with my hand and pressed my fingers toward the king, then shook them. In an instant, the king vanished, and the leaf rot rearranged itself into nothing. But in that moment, as my hand touched the warm, thick pocket of water where the king had been, I was seized by an irrepressible happiness, more giddy than any stolen wine or dentist's gas had ever made me. Darby stuck in his hand too and I saw his lips curl into a smile around his snorkel. As much as we liked to search for the kings, it was this brief moment of joy that drew Darby and me to the quarry floor. We were addicted to this essence.

Out of air again, we swam to the surface.

"That was a good one," he said, still smiling.

"Best yet." We had found several tucked into the spaces between the granite slabs. We had gone through everything we could think of to explain them. They were wooden statues that had rotted. They were skeletons of animals swept up in the flood or catfish tainted by mercury. They were made of clay thinned by years in the water. Other kids had made them as a joke. But nothing explained the electric charge that ran through our hands when they touched that warmth at the bottom of the cold quarry. We had tried to raise one to the surface, but brought up only a handful of leaves, translucent in the summer sun.

We gave up trying to explain the kings or to bring them home to show our father. We just assumed we would understand someday. Until then, we simply looked for the kings and touched them, felt the pulsing warmth they held spread through us. I suppose it was wrong, but being boys, our first notion when we found something unusual was to destroy it.

"Ready?" Darby asked. I nodded.

We dove that afternoon until our lungs ached. The brown world of the quarry bottom had started to seem familiar as the dark rooms of our house at night. But for all our searching, we found nothing. We pulled ourselves reluctantly from the water in time to be home for dinner.

At that age, much was unexplained. Why had our mother moved back to Richmond? Why hadn't Darby and I gone with her? Why wouldn't our father explain why they separated? Then there were the many intertwined mysteries of women and sex and life and the world beyond our town. Finding the kings at the bottom of the quarry was a gift, inexplicable but real, a secret that my brother and I hoarded all through the long summer after the flood.

By August, I could shake my head and hear water sloshing. When I pressed hard, quarry water dripped from my ears. It stained my pillow brown as tobacco juice. I didn't tell my father, who would know where we had been swimming. Instead, I let my world gradually turn quiet. The sounds faded slowly, until finally Darby had to look straight at me when he spoke for me to understand him. He begged me not to tell. He had me hop on one foot for hours, trying to clear out the fluid the way we did at the pool. It didn't work.

The pressure inside my head was almost unbearable and I had to stuff my ears with cotton to keep the tobacco juice from leaking. I played the piano one last long afternoon. All the songs of the world flowed out my fingers and across the keys of our upright. I was so deafened that the piano made no sound to me. I heard only my own distant humming, as if I were singing at the bottom of the quarry. At the end of the day, I turned myself in, handing my father a note that explained it all. His mouth moved angrily as he read, then he peered into my ears with a flashlight, then took me to the doctor, who did the same thing with a small silver instrument that hurt. I was diagnosed with a severe infection of the middle ear.

During the drive to Washington the next morning, my father reached back occasionally to slap Darby, who took most of the blame for this particular episode. We had a steak dinner downtown; then the next morning I had a brief surgery. By that afternoon, I could hear again, the sounds so loud and unexpected that I had to clamp my hands over my ears to filter them. I've forgotten the details now—how long I was in surgery, if it hurt or not, going home. What I remembered was the watery silence.

DAY 35. *He is very angry.* Nin wrote on a child's toy. She pulled the plastic up and the words disappeared, then handed me the slate and the red plastic pen.

I wrote nothing for a moment, struggling to hold the small pen in my hands. I remembered that it was called a magic slate. Nin watched, her eyes unchanged by sympathy. She had grown accustomed to my condition.

Get me out of here! I scrawled, then shoved the slate back to her. She pulled the plastic up and my words disappeared.

You'll be leaving soon, she wrote. *I promise.*

I took the slate and erased it. *Did I hurt him very badly?*

No, it only made him angry, Nin scribbled.

I thought of a bullfight Maura and I had seen in Seville decades ago, when we visited during the spring *feria*. The picadors had administered the first wounds, which incited the bull to charge and be quickly killed by a short, nonchalant toreador with a pockmarked face. In all, it took a few unremarkable minutes, and Maura and I had left feeling short-changed yet grateful. Rather than wait for the next fight, we escaped out to the street, where we found a corner bar and drank manzanilla and ate salt-baked fish. My own ordeal had stretched out for weeks now, the wounds administered but not the *coup de grace*.

Angry enough to kill me? I wrote.

Non! Nin wrote emphatically. *We are working to get you released. Our faction is mobilizing.* A black snake lowered and she quickly pulled up the plastic to erase the slate.

One of the aliens ran into the room, his mask almost falling off. Two others chased him and tackled him on the floor just a few feet away. He carried a small square of cardboard. As they struggled, he kept trying to hold the cardboard toward the ceiling. I couldn't read the message.

Nin watched as he was dragged back through the apartment by his arms.

Who was that? I wrote, then handed her the slate.

One of your supporters, she wrote. *Someone who thinks this has gone on long enough.*

Are there more of them?

Nin nodded. *But there are just as many who feel strongly that we should continue.*

I pulled the slate out of her hand and threw it over in the corner. It fluttered down to the floor. Nin's mouth moved but I had no idea what she was saying, nor did I care. I put my hands over my ears to stop the painful roaring of air. Nin kept talking, standing closer to me now. Behind her scarf, her eyes flashed with anger. She was wrong. She wasn't the jailer who handed me the keys. She kept me in jail with hope and promises and expectations. For weeks I had waited for just the right moment so she could help me outsmart Blackbeard. He didn't seem to be particularly brilliant to me, but Nin was no match for him. He was, after all, a fanatic.

"Go away!" I screamed. With each hour, my memory of how to say words seemed to fade. I was no longer sure that what I thought I was saying matched what came out of my mouth.

Nin turned and rushed out of the room. I threw a chair and a bottle of mineral water after her. I still waited to hear the crash, half-closed my eyes against it. But the bottle shattered silently on the floor.

DAY 36. A pair of eyes stared from the windowsill, one blue eye and one green eye, slightly crossed, just inches apart. I screamed and moved away from them. The two eyeballs glistened beneath the bright lights. Moving closer, I could see that they were glass. I picked up the green one and found it surprising heavy. I took the blue one in my other hand. An eye in either ruined hand. A Dali painting. They were beautiful, in a way, the milky white joining the clear section at the front with a seamless flow. I stared at them for quite while, examining them with my own eyes. Then I realized what they were for.

I held the eyes up to the black snakes, let the world see them. "Do you find this amusing?" I shouted. "Is the world so sick that you find it amusing? Imagine that it was your own eyes that were going to be ripped out. Imagine that if you can."

When the quarry water filled my middle ears, I had welcomed its warm silence. But now my deafness frustrated me. I couldn't be sure I was speaking clearly. I couldn't be sure I was saying anything at all.

I tightened my fingers around the eyeballs and drew back my arm to throw them.

A hand grabbed my wrist and stopped me. I turned to find Blackbeard shaking his head. He carefully pulled each of the eyeballs out of my hand and cradled them in his palm. He rubbed the fingers of his other hand together, indicating that these were expensive.

"Thanks, thanks a lot," I said. "I appreciate your going to such trouble."

Blackbeard shrugged. He said something, but I couldn't tell what it was. I squinted toward him. He rolled his eyes, as if my deafness was an affectation. He took a pen from his pocket and walked over to the white wall.

Tomorrow, these eyes will be yours.

I shook my head. "No!"

He nodded. *They are of high quality,* he wrote. *Taken directly from a hospital.* He rolled the eyes slightly in his hand, a magician palming quarters.

"No!" I shouted again. I shoved him against the wall and tried to get the pen from him. Thinking I wanted to write something, Blackbeard handed it to me. I pulled the pen back and shoved it as hard as I could into his thick middle.

He pushed me away and raised his black sweater. I saw a small red welt on the white skin of his belly. He touched it carefully to see if it was bleeding. Satisfied that no harm was done, he pulled down his sweater and straightened it. Then he rushed across the room and shoved me until I was backed against the wall, his big hands pressing my shoulders.

He shouted, spittle flying, but I couldn't understand.

I said nothing.

Again, he took out a pen from his pocket, this time keeping it as far from me as possible.

I turned my head to read what he had written. *The votes are in. We proceed. One final level and then you're free.*

"Free!" I shouted. "You're going to cut my eyes out. You're crazy. You're all crazy!"

He shrugged, then wrote again. *Our actions have been called brilliant by some, perverse by others. But we have been original. We have captured the attention of the world.*

"Then leave me alone," I shouted. "If you have a shred of human kindness, leave my eyes. You've taken everything else."

Blackbeard shook his head, then wrote on the wall. *There is a unity that we must achieve. Only then will our mission be judged a success. We must teach the world that this is what happens to apologists for globalization . . .*

Blackbeard kept writing but I didn't read on. His rants were as uninteresting written as they were delivered aloud.

"You're actually going to cut out my eyes? Is such cruelty part of your program, your ideology?"

He shook his head and chose another place on the white wall to write. *They won't be cut out. Just removed and replaced.* He held up the eyeballs in his hand.

"That isn't the sort of operation that . . . it's a different thing than before . . . you can't do it, you just can't." My mind raced. I thought of the blind boy in Simms, his pink fingers running over the lead soldiers.

Blackbeard shook his head and wrote. *It won't be a problem. Removing an eye is easy. All it takes is a confident man and a coffee spoon.*

At that moment the lights dimmed and went out completely. We stood in the darkened room. Blackbeard rushed back to the entrance. I leaned against the wall and stared into the dark, wondering if this was my induction into blindness, waiting just a day away. The lights came on again. The destroyed room was filled with its familiar debris, the walls thick with Blackbeard's words.

DAY 37. Fear took hold. When this night was over, the Doctor would come one last time. I paced the rooms, the black snakes following me. I smashed furniture. I turned over the futon and made a barrier of it against the door. I took Blackbeard's cheap pen and wrote on the wall of my innocence, begged anyone who could read my words to do something, anything to stop what was about to happen.

The insatiable audience waited, safe behind computer screens. Their eyes weren't scheduled for plucking. Their lives were not at risk. Those more guilty than I could ever be went unjudged, unpunished, and my anger at them burned. There was no justice in what was happening to me.

As the sun brightened the windows, I fell asleep with the full weight of dread on my shoulders, sure of what the next day would bring. Blackbeard kept his promises.

DAY 38. By evening, I had heard nothing from Blackbeard or the others. No food arrived. Nin didn't rescue me. The Doctor didn't come with his bag. I raged through the apartment, screaming up at the ceiling. The snakes scattered at my approach.

The air thrummed with silence. I wanted to hear my footsteps again, or the sound of my own voice, shouting again in the empty apartment.

"I demand to be released!" I shouted. "This whole ordeal has gone on too long and you know it. Maybe you joined this group thinking it was a good chance to protest American domination. Fine. Your points are important and you've taken them to the world. But what you're doing now is torture, pure and simple. It is the work of madmen. If you have any shred of . . ."

The red lights flickered off, then the room lights. I stood in the dim apartment for a moment. The whitewashed windows turned dark, and with this darkness I spun from a powerful vertigo. I stood on top of a very tall building on a starless night, unsure where the roof ended. I swayed for a moment, then knelt on the floor, my forehead on the cool wood. Even then, the floor careened. I turned to the side to let a stream of water and white lumps of day-old rice spray from my mouth. Putting my hands on the floor did nothing to stop the room's gyroscopic spinning. They felt nothing.

I pulled my sleeve up and pressed my forearm against the floor. With my forehead and my arm against the floor I could give the darkness two points that I could be sure of—two points that drew a line across the floor. I stood, but the swaying began again. I turned back into a shuffling crab, moving into the corner where the futon once was. Here I stayed for hours, half-sleeping, lost. This was what it was going to be like after the Doctor replaced my eyes with the blue and green forgeries. I would be forever lost in a blackened gyre, a realization that made me panic even further, muttering a prayer into the floor to make it stop, willing the wood to rise up and protect me.

The lights came back on and I could see the destroyed apartment again, the futon still pushed up against the door, the trash piled deep along the edges of the room. The black snakes flickered on. No one came in to explain. Most likely, the darkness was a technical problem, solved now, enabling the audience to see me sitting cross-legged on the floor, eyes darting from place to place, watching it all.

) ♩ ♪ ♩ ♩ ♪ ♩) ♩♪♩)) ♩♪ ♩ ♩ ♪ ♪♩ ♪♩ ♪ ♩ ♩ ♪♩♪ ♩ ♩ ♪ ♩ ♩ ♪ ♩ ♩ ♪ ♪

DAY 39. I dreamt of the silence at the bottom of the quarry, so different from the silence here in the apartment. There the water blanketed the body, protecting it in its womb. Here I sensed that all sound had been ripped away from the earth. Silence brought the emptiness of January afternoons, the blue sky fading, a frigid wind stripping the city. *When will this all end?*

I woke slowly to the sound of voices.

"And there's eleven left on the first . . ." a man said urgently.

"Find out what time . . . taken from the old . . ." said a woman.

The voices cycled in and out of earshot, a radio playing in a swerving car.

" . . . and that was when I noticed that the . . ." said another man.

Then the first woman again. "It builds up year after year and then . . ."

Then nothing. I sat up on the floor, the room dim and empty. I rubbed my ears and heard nothing. I looked around the room and saw no one. Where were the voices coming from? Did the Black Hats have so much technology on hand that they could beam these voices directly into my mind? Or was I finally breaking down after more than a month of boredom and terror?

Blackbeard arrived at noon on a bright orange plastic plank, the kind used to carry accident victims from wreckage. Six aliens shuffled forward, bearing him into the room Cleopatra-style. Blackbeard held out the two glass eyes like ripened plums. His mouth moved, of course, but I could hear nothing and was glad for a fleeting moment that I couldn't.

Behind him came the Doctor and Nin, both looking straight ahead without a glance at me. The Doctor's unbuttoned white coat was marked with dirt and splattered with brown bloodstains. He looked at me for a moment and shook his head in resignation, as if to tell me that he didn't want to be here either, but that nothing he or anyone else had done could stop this inevitable afternoon. I almost welcomed the arrival of this inane procession, if only to end the waiting.

The aliens put down the board and Blackbeard rolled off and swayed a little as he stood. He walked over to the wall.

Please lie on the board and we will begin, he wrote in foot-high letters.

I ran past him into the other room. The aliens were close behind me. I turned at the whitened window and swung at the first one to get close, sending his mask spinning across the room. He lay in the corner for a moment, stunned, hands over his face. I held my throbbing hand. The blow had cracked the hardened surface and a drop of amber fluid slid down my wrist onto the floor.

The alien struggled to put his mask back on. He was just a kid, maybe sixteen or seventeen. His black hair was cut short in a military style which did little to toughen his soft, pale face. He looked up one last time, narrowing his eyes at me, sending out a palpable hatred. What made him so angry? Was it what I had done years ago? Or was it the fact that he was no longer anonymous and protected? The world would know his face the same way it knew mine.

The others grabbed me and carried me into the room, where the board lay across two metal chairs. As I fought with all the strength left in me, they forced me down and fastened my wrists and ankles with tight straps, then tightened a final strap over my waist. I tried to lift my legs and arms but couldn't. Thrashing as hard as I could only allowed me to raise my chest an inch. In the circle above me, I saw Blackbeard looking down at me from one side, the Doctor on the other. At the edges hovered a scrim of aliens. Above them all, the black snakes swayed, red lights burning.

"Don't do this!" I screamed.

Blackbeard blinked. He took the two glass eyes and polished each on his black sweater for a moment. He handed them carefully to the Doctor, who put them carefully in the pocket of his lab coat. He took a syringe from the other pocket and held it up for a moment, eyebrows raised above his Zorro mask. I tried to knock it away. The needle stung my arm and a slow warmth spread almost immediately.

They waited for a moment for the shot to work its way deeper. My arms turned heavy almost immediately and I had to fight to keep my eyes open.

Blackbeard waved one of the aliens forward, the angry boy whose mask I had just knocked off. Blackbeard reached into his shirt pocket and held up a shining coffee spoon. He handed it to the alien he had chosen to be my surgeon. As he walked toward me, I saw the boy's blank eyes behind the mask. His shaking hand came closer to my eyes, the spoon glinting in the bright room. In its rounded bottom, I saw my own face, eyes wide, mouth held tight in a rictus of fear. I turned to the side but eager hands reached out to hold me.

Nin shouted something else, two words, it seemed, and there was a sudden lull, a caesura that held the room still for a moment. The aliens at the edges, Blackbeard and Nin close together, the Doctor nearby. Once again, we found ourselves in an absurd still life, so strange but familiar.

Blackbeard grabbed Nin and pushed her in front of him. The room erupted in chaos. The aliens fought each other, fists pulling off masks, bottles flying, new aliens swarming in. Above it all, the black snakes glowed, recording every moment. After what seemed like a long struggle, Blackbeard came closer, holding Nin's arm twisted behind her back. He reached down and unzipped my trousers, then pulled them roughly around my knees. I struggled, but the straps held me. Blackbeard shoved Nin's head down and I could see her screaming over and over. Behind the scarf, her eyes were wild with anger. She tossed her narrow shoulders back and forth trying to get free, but Blackbeard kept pushing her forward until I could feel her fast breathing on my thighs.

Through the painkillers, I realized what was happening. Blackbeard loved the grand gesture, the photogenic moment that would keep our audience entertained. He wanted to introduce a trace of pornography to our predictable tableau of violence and torture. What could be more exciting to our audience than to watch my eyes plucked out while Nin took my cock in her mouth? What could be more completely over the top?

Blackbeard looked at me for a long moment, eyes lively, a naughty schoolboy. A concussion shook the room and a warm shower rained down on us all. Blackbeard recoiled against the wall, eyes open, blood rushing from the mouth hole of his mask. The aliens ran to him and pressed their hands over the cavern at the back of his head, trying to stop the blood with their hands. He slid down to the floor.

The Doctor waved them away with Blackbeard's silver pistol. I struggled to sit up. I twisted my head to see Nin, not sure where she had gone. The Doctor kicked at the last aliens and they were gone, leaving Blackbeard wide-eyed and still, blood dripping from his mask.

The room was still for a moment.

"Untie me," I shouted, struggling against the ropes.

The Doctor put the pistol in the pocket of his lab coat and stood over me for a moment. Nin appeared at his side, calm, at ease even. She bent down, then reappeared again. She held the silver spoon's handle delicately between her thumb and forefinger.

I screamed. Nin wasn't the jailor who would hand me the key. There was no key, just the coffee spoon swinging back and forth in her fingers.

"How could you lie to me!" I shouted, then realized how foolish this question was. The lie was my own. I had been drawn in by her quiet ways, so different from Blackbeard, so much like my own. She had given me false hope, and I had willingly taken it and multiplied it a hundredfold until it actually seemed possible that she would help me.

She handed the spoon to the Doctor, who fixed his dark gaze on me. He reached toward me with the spoon, which grew larger and larger and then doubled. I squeezed my eyes closed, then felt a twinge in my right eye as he wedged the spoon's edge between my eyelids. I struggled against the cool, sharp metal. A deep wave of pain swept over me and then the ceiling swayed wildly as he urged the right eyeball free and gently raised it higher and higher. The pain turned the room deep green and blurry. I couldn't breathe.

As the room darkened, I took one final glimpse of the world.

While the Doctor worked, his hands slow and unwavering, Nin stood still, head bowed as if in prayer. Nin was the first person I saw in my prison and she would be the last. Another sharp twinge and the world turned black, taking with it Nin, the deceiver, and the Doctor, the confident man with a coffee spoon.

♪♪ ♪♪♪♪♪ ♪ ♪♪♪ ♪ ♪♪♪♪♪♪♪♪♪♪ ♪♪♪♪♪♪♪ ♪♪ ♪♪♪♪♪♪

DAY 40. I woke struggling. A low peak of pain throbbed behind my eyes. My mind was still fogged by painkillers. One hand had come untied and I reached up to find my head wrapped in a thick layer of bandages. In darkness or blindness, I wasn't sure which, I untied my other hand with quick, desperate tugs at the ropes, then reached down to free my waist and ankles. I rolled off the orange board and onto the floor, sending the pain blazing.

I tore away the soft gauze wrapped around my head, unwrapping it as quickly as I could. After the gauze came two thick pads that covered each eye. I peeled back the pad on the right eye slowly. I could see nothing. Reaching up to it, I felt the hard glass beneath my eyelid, the searing in the socket. I threw the bandages on the floor and screamed as loudly as I could, hearing nothing, feeling only the electric vibration.

My fingers peeled back the edge of the pad that covered my left eye slowly. I saw my thickened fingers holding the bandage, then dropped it and watched it fall next to me. The eye was soft and warm, free of any pain. I blinked at the familiar disarray of the apartment. I laughed, so relieved that for a moment I forgot everything around me. For some reason, the efficient, reliable Doctor hadn't completed his final task. Did he take pity on me? Or was his work interrupted?

I looked around the room, the fast shifting of my head making the right side of my face throb. The lights were on full and all of the snakes hung limply from the ceiling. Blackbeard slumped against the wall, chin bearded black with crisp dried blood. He had died with one arm half raised, his mouth open, mid-scream. His silver pistol rested on his lap. I thought of trying to pick it up and fire another shot between his eyes.

I reached out and pulled away his mask, letting it drop to the floor. I had waited so long for this moment. Blackbeard's face was pale and speckled, his beard untrimmed, his nose long and noble. He was younger than I had expected. He looked completely normal, an assistant professor, a waiter at a coffeehouse, a musician.

I pulled back my leg and kicked him in the belly as hard as I could, sending his body slumping slowing to the floor, a statue of flesh, head wobbling.

For weeks I had dreamed of revenge, of giving Blackbeard at least some of the pain he had brought to me. He had tortured me. But it was Nin who betrayed me, Nin who told the Doctor to continue. I could still see the shining spoon dangling from her fingers.

I left Blackbeard and stumbled to the bathroom to look in the mirror. My blue glass eye was sunken and smaller than my real eye. It stared off to one side. A thin trail of blood dripped from the corner and down my face. I pressed the gauze pad back over the ruined eye.

I walked on, left eye forward, arms stretched out before me, a cyclops roaming slowly through the empty apartment, flat as a painting. Ahead waited the white door I had kicked, the door that I had dreamed of walking through for so long. It was open wide.

I walked slowly toward it, unsure that anything I saw was what I thought it was. I waited for the Doctor to walk out from behind the door, ready to finish his task. One final ordeal. But no one stopped me.

The next room was huge as a warehouse and dimly lit by glowing computer screens on a row of desks. Cables sagged from the high ceiling and the floor was thick with paper. I could see the back of my apartment walls, the boards nailed into the cement floor. It was no more real than a stage set.

I walked around to see the whitened windows. In front of them, a high-intensity bulb moved along an arc of wire. This false sun had lit my days. Numbers scrawled along aluminum marked the time—14 *heures* . . . 16 *heures*. Beneath the sun was a large, detailed painting of a hazy world seen from a distance. Clouds hovered over the dim landscape of factories and fields. Here were the smokestacks I had seen when I managed to scrape off some of the paint. I shook my head. My ordeal was all as unreal as this set, the painted landscape, the lightbulb sun. But when I raised my hands, I could see they were still hardened and thick. When I turned my head, I could still feel the pain behind the socket where the glass eye now rolled. When I kicked over the painted world and smashed the sun, I heard nothing.

I walked around to the other side of the set and into a smaller, dim room filled with more desks, some overturned, others topped by computer terminals, still glowing. An alien lay slumped at one, his fingers still on the bloody keyboard. Perhaps he had been one of the dissenters, one of the ones who wanted to stop it all. He could have been the voice I heard coming from the ceiling.

On the screen, I saw my own screaming face and a clock with numbers that revolved. *Jours. 40. Heures. 13. Minutes. 7. Seconds.* The numbers blurred by, tallying my imprisonment.

Another terminal showed a large photo of me, taken early in my imprisonment, when my hands were still my own, when I could hear and taste and smell. I was still wearing my white shirt and dark trousers from my last civilized dinner. How long ago this seemed, and how different the man I saw on the screen was from the one that reached toward it. When my finger touched the monitor, words scrolled across. *The hands, unfeeling to the needs of the rest of the world.* Then a small box appeared on the screen and a movie began to play. I saw the Doctor hunched over my hands, scraping them over and over with the cheese grater. My mouth was open in a silent scream, and Blackbeard sat to one side smoking a cigarette. So this was what the world had been watching. I shoved the monitor off the desk and it shattered on the floor.

Across the room, I saw a door with *Ingang* stenciled above it in red. I walked toward it slowly, left eye forward, stepping over fallen desks and scattered files. I walked faster. But at the door, I stopped, my hands on the silver bar that would push the door open. I turned to look back through the office, the false apartment, abandoned now by everyone but me. Then I turned to look at the door carefully, sure that when I finally opened the door, it would explode and kill me, a fiery, ironic finale, the last laugh. But I couldn't stop myself from pushing.

I felt a cold breeze. The door flew open wide and I saw a narrow street. It was dusk and businessmen moved quickly along the sidewalk in their dark coats, legs blurring. I stepped out, wrapping my arms around me. People barged past, not noticing a stunned man with a bandaged eye, wearing only a blood-splotched white shirt and thin trousers on a cool evening. I knew I should seek someone out, should stop them and signal for help. But I found myself on the edge of the crowd with the beggars and children, unable to weave my way into it.

The businessmen looked so perfect, their dark coats swaying at their knees. Some wore hats or carried briefcases. Others had leather gloves or carried parcels tied in string. Once I would have been among them, walking back to my flat, a paper-wrapped bottle from the wine shop under my arm. Their flow through the city was a silent ballet to me, distant and beautiful. I didn't want to interrupt it. Or join it.

I walked past the store windows filled with headless mannequins in expensive suits, past a shop where a bored woman in a black apron measured out cheese on a scale. Behind me stood the dark tower of the central bank, ahead I saw a cavernous train station where people streamed out of an archway. *Centrum,* one of the street signs read. I found a certain satisfaction at knowing that I was in downtown Antwerp on a cool fall night. Though anchored in time and place, my mind raced. I stopped at a kiosk lined with posters and leaned my left eye forward to read about new plays, art shows, political rallies. That I could stand here and read felt like such freedom. No one was watching me. I could hear no one. If I closed my left eye, the world disappeared.

I recognized this street as the Meir, the city's expensive shopping district. I had come here once to buy Maura a pair of diamond earrings for our anniversary. I had spent a morning searching in vain for a legendary chocolate shop tucked in an alley near here.

It was turning darker, and the lights inside the stores took on an orange glow. As I walked, I held my hand to half-shield my eye. It was impossible for me to look at anything for very long. Streetlights, stores, people—it was all too rich to take in at once.

On the right, a side street veered away from the crowded Meir and I walked down it, eye focused carefully on the cobblestones in front of me. I savored each breath of cool night air. I shivered for a moment, then smiled. To shiver again after the dead warm air of the apartment was a luxury. I imagined seeing myself from above, a bandaged man walking down a narrow street, one eye taped closed, the other hungry and roving. Certainly I stood out, but no one stopped me, and I had no need to stop them. For weeks I had dreamed of running out of my cell and finding the first person I came to and . . . and what? Ask for help? On my own, I had survived forty days that might have killed another man. I didn't need their help.

I came to a small park, where a path wound past garden beds neatly cut back for the winter. I stood in front of a tall statue of a stout, proud-looking man carrying a sheath of grain. *Jan Peeters, Botaniste, 1599.* I sat on a wooden bench beneath Mijnheer Peeter's benevolent gaze. Above, the first stars pierced the indigo sky. I leaned back and closed my eye. The cyclops at rest. How few times in my life would there be a time like this, a moment of total freedom?

For weeks, my imprisonment and suffering had been on display to the world. Now no one knew where I was. I had no responsibilities or fears. I heard nothing, though I imagined there were people walking past the park, low Flemish voices echoing along the cobblestones. I could smell nothing, though the cooling air was surely redolent with earth and leaves. My eye was closed, but I knew that the sky was fading quickly, giving way to night.

Freed from it all, I discerned the first glimmer of another order beyond the city's weave of streets and buildings. I perceived, though my eye was closed, a small blue fire waiting in the distance. I would have to walk along the riverbanks and dive into the deep water to find it. I would have to swim to the bottom and push my deadened hands into the burgeoning rot to hold it. But I would feel the heat of that blue fire, closer and closer still.

An insistent finger tapped on my shoulder. I opened my eye and saw a young blond woman in a long green coat. When I looked at her, her eyes widened and she gave a silent scream. She waved frantically and shouted. I closed my eye again. It was too late.

Suddenly I was surrounded by people, their faces peering down at me, some curious, others frightened. The small park turned crowded with businessmen, women, a young boy in a fur hat. More people pressed close, knocking me off the bench. An old man shouted down at me but I shook my head and pointed to my ears. One of the businessmen took out a silver pen and wrote on the brilliant white cuff of his shirt. *Are you Eliott Gast?*

I stared at the crowd of faces, my audience, and nodded slowly. Yes, I was Eliott Gast. They stared at me with concern and surprise, spoke urgently and silently among themselves. Then they lifted me from the ground and carried me down the narrow street on their shoulders—a one-eyed man, a king.

Thanks foremost to Juris Jurjevics, never in the shadow of giants. Thanks also to Joel Achenbach, Peter Broderick, Bill Ciccariello, Cristina Concepcion, Michael Congdon, Jack Engler, Patrick Gypen, Charles van Hoorick, Gene Hunt, Craig Moodie, Clark Quin, James Reyman, and my family and friends. Special thanks to the Concord (Massachusetts) Free Public Library.